T0209730

With Angels Like Peg, Who Needs Gabriel?

H. R. Davis

BALBOA.
PRESS

A DIVISION OF HAY HOUSE

Balboa Press books may be ordered through booksellers or by contacting:

Balboa Press
A Division of Hay House
1663 Liberty Drive
Bloomington, IN 47403
www.balboapress.com
1 (877) 407-4847

Print information available on the last page.

ISBN: 978-1-9822-3189-7 (sc)
ISBN: 978-1-9822-3193-4 (e)

Balboa Press rev. date: 07/22/2019

Contents

The Value of Seaglass 1

Dancing Demons on the Table 8

The Unheard, Unfounded, Unearthed Existence
      of the Piggopotomus 12

The Legend of the Suicide Queen 20

The Death of Mr. Simms 30

The Legend of Peg 47

Two Lost Boys 71

A Really Safe Place 88

The Value of Seaglass

The small boy sat patiently across the table from the very old man. The boy must have been no more than twelve, his shaggy brown hair stood in every direction atop his round baby face. His recent growth spurt left his clothes clinging tightly to his lanky body. His enormous blue eyes looked intently at the very old man.

The small room smelled heavily of tobacco smoke and stale grease. The coffee shop wasn't exactly a coffee shop, but a hangout spot on rainy days for the ancient residents of the small coastal town. It did serve coffee and advertised with a new sign on the street that coffee and scones were sold here. It used to be a fisherman's pub and the ancient patrons still sought the stale cheap whiskey for which the place used to be known and thus the barista kept a good stock of cheap alcohol behind the bar.

The small boy was visiting with is parents some ancient family member who lived in the small town by the bay. His parents had told him to go to the shore and hunt for shells or to go explore somewhere nearby, but mostly to get out of their way. Even at his young age, he was completely used to being neglected and honestly, he was more than happy to get out of the dark house that confined the ancient relative

1

he had come to visit. His room was in the attic, accessible only by a small ladder and trap door in the upstairs hallway. There was a bed and a nightstand and a small lamp beside a clouded window. His parents stayed downstairs in the only true bedroom and the ancient aunt slept on a rollaway in the living room next to her table of meds. The entire house smelled of dank musty mold and vicks. There were machines in the kitchen with tubes and wires that ran around the corner to the old aunt's bed. It was an untidy and unwholesome place. The small boy was vaguely aware that the smell of death was as present as his parents were absent.

Today his parents were downtown visiting the town's only lawyer and he was left to his own devices. He had wandered down to the shore and when the rain started falling, he headed back towards the ancient aunt's house. But a sudden downpour had pushed him into this small coffee bar, an ancient building with dark stained glass, stained darker by smoke and old grease. The furniture was dark wood, and the floors were black, with fresh sawdust swirling in the corners. Upon entering, the small boy was greeted by the barman and he asked for a hot chocolate. He pushed a fresh $20 across the dark bar and was greeted with some change. He had meant to sit at the table by the window, so he could see when the rain stopped, but the very ancient man in a dark corner motioned him over. There were no introductions, there was no small talk. The old man simply threw several pieces of colored glass onto the table, the glass was sea glass and was worn completely smooth by decades of being tossed against the sand and the rocks at the seashore.

The small boy looked up at the old man with very large

eyes, the old man, looked at the small boy through tiny slits in his face behind which sat old cataract covered eyes. He smiled a one-sided smile, evidence of a stroke years ago. He sat uneasily as if his chair legs were all different lengths and he waited for the small boy's full attention before he began to speak. The small boy looked at the pieces of glass on the table and when the old man laughed and nodded, he picked them up cautiously and felt the dull rounded edges. He admired the muted transparency of some and struggled to make out the color of others in the darkness of the unlit corner of the bar. The old man pointed at the pieces in the small boy's hand and the boy set them cautiously back on the table. "Them's sea glasses" the old man whispered.

The small boy sat silent and looked intently at the old man who shifted again on his unsteady chair. He ran dark heavy fingers through his unkempt grey beard. "We's all sea glasses boy." He spoke confidently as if he had rehearsed this speech a hundred times and knew exactly where to pause for effect. The barman moved to the end of the bar, closer to where the very old man and the small boy sat in the corner. The barman had heard the story a hundred times before and while he wasn't particularly fond of the old man, the stories were good for business. Tourist would flock to the old man for a story from an authentic local.

The very old man picked up a water glass from the table and set it in front of the boy for effect. "We all starts a' sometin' else, sometin' complete and sound. We all starts as a bottle or glass or sometin' recognizable, sometin' you's can fill up with love and friendship and life."

Then he removed the water glass and replaced it with the broken shards of seaglass.

"We all starts as sometin' new and some of we stays that way, new and shiny and complete. But mosts of we gets broken. We is fragile things, boy." He stopped and sucked in a deep breath as though it pained him to breath. The boy, eyes full of wonder, listened unmoved from his dirty old dark chair. His hot chocolate, now barely warm sat in front of him untouched since the old man started speaking.

"At first we's broken and we's sharp and no one wants to handle we's else theys gets cut. But then we's get washed around in the sea of life and the sharpness wears away as we be thrown on the rocks and washed over by the trials of life. Then we's be getting broken again, into smaller and smaller pieces, we's just a piece of what we used to be, most us pieces be lost to the waves and again, the sharpness wear offs."

At this point, the very old man stood up with great effort and with great help from a thick cane, he moved to the bar and the barman refilled his water glass. The old man shakily made his way back to the table, his water spilling as he went. The rain outside had subsided after one last torrent that had shaken the windows and left a small stream leaking in under the door to the place. The boy sat in silence waiting for the very old man to return. He looked at the small colored pieces of glass on the table and thoughtlessly picked one up, rubbing it between his forefinger and his thumb, feeling the edges that had once been sharp as razors but had been worn smooth by years of being beaten by the waves. The old man returned to his shaky chair and set his water in front of himself.

"Pick one you think is pretty, boy." He said, losing his seaman accent for a moment. "Even tho we be broken, the wear we gets from hard life gives we beauty again. We be

4

smaller bits of our first selves, but we been through the waves and comes out as something pretty and desirable again."

The boy looked at the small pieces, some as small as baby teeth, others as large as quarters, all worn and smooth, none sharp or dangerous. He pondered at which he might take, this was truly a treasure, something he could take back home with him and show his classmates at school. Something that would make this trip to the coast worth the disappointment. He suddenly picked up a blue piece of glass, a triangle of beauty, small, but precious.

"Aye, a grand choosing!" the old man exclaimed. "Truly you picked a rare piece, blue glass be hard to find." The small boy held the small piece of glass in the palm of his left hand and rubbed it gently with the fingers of his right hand. It was the color of his eyes. A small tear appeared in the corner of one eye. It wasn't normal for him to receive gifts from anyone. His parents never would have given him such a treasure as this. He wiped his eye and looked up at the old man with a grateful expression on his face. The old man met his eye and a look of surprise appeared on his dirty old face. His story had never meant so much to anyone before and this boy seemed genuinely grateful for this unexpected gift.

"Remember boy, we's all glass, we's gets broke and polished by life, but we's still has value and beauty. Ain't en nothin' when we's young that can prepare we's for what us will be when we's old. We's treasure inside us all en it only taken the right soul to be seein that."

The small boy looked up from his new treasure and looked at the very old man who sat back in his chair, his dirty old hands crossed across his chest, a half smile on his face. The very old man reached down and carefully picked up the remaining pieces of glass from the table and put them in the breast pocket of his vest. "I thank ye for yern time and fer listenin to an old man fer a bit." He spoke slowly to the boy in an almost dismissive tone. His voice cracked a bit as the small boy closed his palm around the new treasure that had been given to him.

For the first time since sitting down, the small boy spoke to the old man. "Thank you for your story and your gift, sir. Perhaps one day my edges will be as polished as yours, perhaps one day I will be a treasure too, just like you." The small boy then stood up from his chair, placed his half full glass of hot chocolate on the bar in front of the bar man and walked briskly out the door.

The very old man sat silently at the table for a few moments and then shakily stood up and made his way to the door, leaving a $5 bill on the bar on his way. He walked into the sunlight outside and the brightness of the sun reflecting off of him was nearly blinding. He disappeared into the brightness of the world and was never seen again at the bar.

The small boy thoughtfully wandered back to his ancient relative's home and found her home alone, sitting, staring blankly into the darkness of her house. He reached out and took her hand. "You're broken," he said to her in a calm voice, "but you're still beautiful and you're a treasure, you've been beaten by life's waves and polished into something you never thought you'd be." As he said this he pressed his new treasure into her hand. She held the glass up feebly and let the light shine through it. She smiled meekly and gave it back to the small boy.

"We're all just sea glass, aren't we?" She chuckled weakly.

The boy nodded his head and held her hand. She smiled at him and then her hand fell limp and she leaned back into her bed. A machine in the next room started beeping and tears welled up in the small boy's eyes. He dropped the small shard of sea glass and heard it make a light "tink" sound as it hit the floor. He sat silently for a few moments, tears streaming down his face, still holding the ancient lady's hand. Then he bent down and picked up his treasure from the floor of the dark, dusty room. He examined it carefully, afraid that it had broken in the fall. It was unharmed and whole. Not just polished by years of wear, but also rendered unbreakable.

Dancing Demons on the Table
"I'll have what he's having"

It's a drizzling rain, it's chilly, typical for Kansas fall weather. But we're inside, sitting across from each other, looking over the menu. Who cares what's on the menu, we didn't really come to eat. We just came from somewhere else, had a few drinks of something, we're stalling, not wasting time at all, but there's more we could be doing instead of this. But this, this is necessary. There are things that we need to say, not to each other, but to ourselves.

We make small talk, looking here and there, commenting on the waiter, the people on the street outside in the drizzling rain, the weather, the décor of the place. I'm comfortable, I barely know him, but I'm comfortable with him. He's older than me in a lot of ways, his age is many years less than mine, but he's travelled more, experienced more, learned more, failed more. He's taken the chances I've never tried, he's worried less, laughed more and lived longer in his years than I ever will.

The food comes, we hardly remember what we ordered, it's not about the food, or the drinks, it's not about getting to know each other, it's about getting to know ourselves. I look up during the conversation and I see into his light eyes. They aren't blue, per say, they are the color of the deepest glacier in Alaska, but they switch to that bluish green of tropical Florida waters. They sparkle with laughter, but they also present a front. They filter his soul. Behind them somewhere is the beauty of a life from long ago, before this condition that has become his life. Now, as I catch a glimpse of them, they shine with sorrow and the tears seem to linger just below the surface. He looks towards the window, avoiding my gaze, I catch a glimpse of pain.

We eat and I'm sure we talked about something, we must have. I don't remember silence, only his golden voice as it flows over the rocks of his life story. And as he speaks to me, I become aware of something I hadn't seen before. He had alluded to it many times, I realize now. He had mentioned things before, but now, somehow it has become necessary to recognize it. His heart is beating, his palms sweat, his hands shake, he takes a drink to calm the demon. His demon will not be calmed, and it reaches out to me. I take a drink, to calm my own demon that I've become so aware is closer to the surface than it has been for a long time.

At the prompt of a choked tear, I start my story. I weave my sadness with my manic silken threads to create a barrier that I've created before many times and worn like a cloak to protect me from the eyes of others, but it's not working. He looks through my disguise. He sees a part of me that is darkness. Others have seen it before, but embarrassed, they look away. Everyone looks away, it's not a pretty darkness, it's not the darkness lit by the moon on a cool summer night. It's a cool darkness, dark as December, cold and clouded, everyone looks away from it. Not him. He stares. His eyes the color of a storm cloud, fierce and unrelenting. A thunder comes from within him and he dives into my darkness, he coaxes my demon from hiding and I fight to hold back the tears. My story of loss, my closeness to the edge, my retreat from family, my seeking of hope in places too dark to find a light switch. He knows that I look for hope in hopeless places because he knows I need to feel that vulnerability to know I'm alive.

I'm sharing lunch with a man and both our demons are on the table, dancing with each other. We talk about aimless things, we cover our shame with smiles, and in the end our demons tire of each other and retreat. We pay the bill, we start to leave, and I resign to the knowledge that I'll never see him again, never talk to him again, never admit that he saw the darkness in my heart and didn't retreat from it. Instead, he reached into it and drug my demons out into the light. They are less powerful now; the light seems to weaken them. I feel like they need more light, and perhaps with enough light the shadows will shrink away. It's ironic that you can't have shadows without light, but in the end, shadows are fleeting, shallow and harmless. They are mirages, wisps of our souls brought out by the light. Shadows are not as bad as the darkness. The darkness is overwhelming, consuming, biding, deep and powerful. It suffocates, it nauseates, it threatens to destroy us.

As I drive home, after leaving him for the day, I start to understand why he's in my life. I know he's temporarily here, just a transient passing through, but I begin to see what he has done for me. No souls cross without leaving a mark one on the other. Sometimes the intersection of these souls changes the course of a life. The destiny of each depends on this nexus, this ley line, this event-horizon. While I cannot see the future, I can see the current direction of my life and I realize that for this strange meeting with the dancing of demons on the table, I'm pointed truer north. I needed him to bring my demon out, in doing so, he lightened my heart, brightened my soul and eased my burden. It didn't take much. Just a lunch at some place I may never go again. I barely remember what I ate and I've forgotten what I drank. But I won't forget his eyes and for a man who carries so much pain, it seems his burden to now carry some of mine. Or maybe he let mine go, I'm not sure where it would go, how it would get there, or what will become of it. But it's not mine to carry anymore. A beautiful young man with a guarded smile and the deepest eyes has unchained me from my darkest thoughts. The sun will shine tomorrow.

I'm told that angels walk among us. They help us when we need it most, push us when we've exhausted our strength and they prompt us to be more human. I'm sure this man is no angel, I know just a portion of where he's been, I know just a few of the things he's done. So, I'm not sure I'll ever run across an angel, but I know there are people in this world that cross your path and you have to stop and get to know them. You have to meet their demons. If you miss these opportunities to learn from them, you miss out on the knowledge, wisdom and love of those far older than you. We shouldn't be afraid, or surprised or expectant of the people we meet. We should embrace them, talk to them, sing with them, live with them and enjoy them while they are here. We do not know which of the people in our lives today may change our tomorrow.

The Unheard, Unfounded, Unearthed Existence of the Piggopotomus
Which is a True and not Fabricated Legendary Beast

In the United States, it is estimated that drowning is the second leading cause of accidental death for children ages 1-14. While the bulk of those drowning deaths are attributed to coastal regions where the waves and currents are feisty, and parents are often in a more lax state of mind, there are some drowning deaths in the rivers, lakes, ponds and marshlands between the Rocky Mountains and the Appalachian Mountains. While many of these inland drownings are the result of negligence and poor supervision, some of them are mysterious and searches do not yield a body. These few deaths may be the direct product of one of the world's most elusive animals: the Piggopotomus.

Once numbering in the hundreds of thousands, this elusive omnivore has declined in number due to deforestation, shared human inhabitation, decline in prey species and the breaking of migration routes caused by man putting up fences, building highways, destroying vast woodland and marsh areas and by the general smell of man which everyone knows is pretty rank. Once the thing of legend among the plain's Native American tribes, this creature has been reduced to the legend of history.

While many don't even believe in the species' existence in the first place, it is understandable that they are placed in the biological literature next to bigfoot and the thunderbird and decent republicans. Mythologists believe that the piggopotomus was never a real species at all, but a product of fairy tales meant to keep tribal children away from the waters. Myths, after all, are meant to explain that which science of the day cannot. One only needs to look to the book of Genesis and the story of Noah and the ark. A terrific story that explains why we have rainbows, it also serves as a historical marker in the history of mankind; a division if you will between pre-history and biblical history. While science can explain the formation of rainbows, followers of the biblical faiths cling to the story of the flood for other reasons. The same holds true for the piggopotomus; children drowning in bodies of water is perfectly explainable: water fills the lungs, displacing oxygen. Unable to process oxygen in the liquid form, the body asphyxiates and shuts down. But then, where are the bodies that are sometimes never found? If you believe in piggopotomi, then you accept the fact that those bodies were consumed by an elusive stealthy beast and the souls of those bodies were separated from the bodies by the strong digestive juices that then turn the bodies into piggopotomus poop.

The stories of these elusive semi-aquatic mammals range geographically from the western slopes of the Appalachians to the eastern foothills of the Rocky Mountains; from as far north as Loring, Montana to the southern marshes of what are now lakes surrounding Hackberry, Louisiana. While accounts differ slightly in description, they all refer to the same species of animal. The Cherokee word for the creature is *amasiqua* which translates to *water – pig*. Other tribes had their own names for the piggopotumus. In the Sauk language used by the Sac and Fox tribes, the creature was called Kishkehkohi Makanaketonwa Kohkosheha which means big-mouthed waterfall pig. No matter the name, the stories are always similar. There's a warning to stay away from the deep water unless you're in a boat.

Similar in detail to the African hippo, the piggopotomus is smaller in size, only up to five or six feet in length, and weighing up to 600 pounds. The two main differences between it and the hippo include the feet and the teeth. Where as hippos have broad, flat feet similar to an elephant with four splayed, webbed toes, the piggo is an even-toed ungulate with two main hooves on each foot, similar to a pig. This cloven hoof makes the footprint indistinguishable from that of a wild boar. The teeth of the piggo are better suited to eating meat than plants, though they are thought to be omnivorous. They possess long, curved saber-shaped canine teeth, similar to that of a saber-tooth tiger. Many believe these canines may be a form of tusk similar to that found in wild pigs and boars of the southern United States, except tusks generally protrude from the lower jaw, not the upper. African hippos are covered in a light hair, as are most animals classified as mammals. Their north American cousins wear a shaggy waterproof coat similar to that of an otter. Their small ears can be folded into themselves to shut off their ear canals from the murky waters. Their eyes are said to provide incredible definition in the muddy waters of the ponds, lakes and rivers they inhabit.

Shy by nature, there have been no confirmed sightings in the last 100 years, historically, however, they were seen by the settlers crossing the plains towards the west. There are a few accounts recorded in diaries and journals of settlers travelling west that describe the creature as a hooved pygmy hippopotamus. An excerpt from a journal by Elizabeth Goodwell wrote about an encounter as her wagon train crossed the Platte River in what is today Western Nebraska.

"August 28, 1841 - Our train of 23 wagons came across a dozen or more creatures that no one had ever seen before. Our Pawnee Indian guide called them 'mud cows' and explained that we should take great caution. Looking like dainty hippos with huge tusks, the furry beasts stalked us and preyed upon several of our livestock. They were sun bathing on the river banks of the Platte River and as we approached, they sprang quickly to their feet as gracefully as butterflies. They submerged into the muddy waters. We stood and watched to see where they would emerge. We caught glimpse of a couple of their nostrils barely breaking the surface. Others stayed submerged for over half an hour at least. We travelled north along the river to find a suitable crossing point for our wagons. One of the mules that the good Doctor Proctor brought with us wandered into the water for relief from the heat. Within seconds and without a sound the mule disappeared into the murky waters with naught but a small splash and some bloody bubbles. We crossed some half a mile upstream, noting the nostrils of the water beasts that followed us upstream. Even in barely three feet of water, they were unnoticeable beneath the surface. My mother, sister and I were huddled in the back of the last wagon to cross and we

watched with horror as a man and his horse that were crossing behind us were pulled beneath the surface in the blink of an eye. Neither were seen again. Thankful to be past that nightmare."

Another story collected from a military journal of Private Jonathan McKenny describes the carnage he witnessed when he and seven other soldiers from Fort Laramie in what is now Southeastern Wyoming, snuck out of the fort and went swimming one hot summer evening.

"June 4, 1851. I was standing on the shore of the small lake, being the last to arrive. The rest of the men were in various forms of undress, most being in the nude. As they entered the water which was as still as a mirror, a small heard of bison approached the opposite bank. A couple of the men were already in the water up to their waist and we all stopped to watch as the enormous creatures entered the water from a small beach area on the far shore, perhaps only two hundred yards to the north of us. There were whispers that we could shoot one and bring it back. Knowing that being caught outside the fort walls, especially after evening chow we would have latrine duty for a month, bringing back a buffalo carcass might save us from punishment.

I reached for my rifle which was in the grass about 4 yards away from me with my knapsack. As we all watched, there was suddenly a great commotion in the water surrounding the bison. It looked as if the surface of the lake reached up and engulfed them. They disappeared silently and quickly beneath the surface. The men that were in the water quickly made for the shore lest they too should be taken. I heard the splashing and shouts from the men behind me as I reached for my rifle. I turned back around to see one Private Jackson pulled under by what looked to be a furry giant pig with saber teeth. There was no sound, nothing but an oily red slick on top of the water. We all ran back to the fort and promised never to tell anyone what we saw. We stood quiet at roll the next morning as Jackson's disappearance was realized. He was branded a deserter and a dispatch was sent back to St. Luis to inform his family of his dishonorable status."

Even Lewis and Clark, on their adventure across the country from St. Luis to the Pacific may have encountered a couple piggos along the way. At one point, the great Newfoundland dog that accompanied them was attacked by a "beaver" which severed an artery in it's hind leg. Such an attack is very uncommon amongst the beaver community and no one on any of the boats reported seeing the offending creature. It sounds much more like a predator looking for a meal. The clean slice of the dog sounds very much like the work of a razor-sharp canine tooth. At another point, they reported something ramming into their great long dugout canoes as if trying to tip them over. Three men went into the water to investigate and only one came back out. The drowning of the two men and the mysterious beasts ramming the boats were attributed to very large paddlefish. (A likely story).

Why are the piggopotomi so elusive? Why are there no bones in the fossil record backing up their existence? Why have none been captured, photographed or recorded in scientific literature?

At face value, those are difficult questions to ponder. However, once one looks at the description of these creatures, it may be easier to explain. These creatures share their habitat with wild boars, some of which are known to read immense sizes. Is it not possible that the bones of the piggopotomi have been mistaken for that of the common boar? Could their bones not be also mistaken for other mammals across the great plains? The only remarkable feature that would set them apart would be those alleged saber teeth. If one were to find one of these giant canine teeth attached to a skull lying beside a river in central Missouri today, it would be written off as some sort of mutated boar or called a hoax because science hasn't accepted the existence of such a creature. I personally can vouch for that story as the one I found which I brought to the University of Missouri in Columbia in 2002. The skull was promptly "lost" and a press release stated that my "find of the century" turned out to be a fabrication using milled elephant tusks, a common pig skull and a giraffe vertebrae. As if I have access to a common pig skull…

Just like bigfoot hairs and scat samples containing DNA that doesn't belong to any known species, the piggopotomus evidence is discarded as a pseudoscience.

If the piggos still exist today, they are most likely to be found across the great plains in rivers, ponds, marshes and lakes. It is believed that they once migrated south in the winter months. An animal that large that lives in the water cannot after all live in the icy conditions of the northern winters. Perhaps there are a few isolated populations left today, lingering around water sources, eating farm animals, wild deer, and anything else they can catch by the watering holes. Perhaps in the dark summer nights in Missouri, their mournful mating call can still be heard, mistaken by scientists as that of a mutated poor-will. Perhaps they come together in forest clearings under the moonlight to perform ancient mating rituals where the males adorn their teeth with moss and the females rub their hairy hides in acres of wild flowers. Perhaps, as a young man wanders through the woods to check his moonshine still he might run across such a clearing and watch, mesmerized for hours as the wild piggos dance around, like fluttering bats, completing their mating orgies before departing and heading their separate ways back to the rivers and the lakes they are used to.

There are many strange things in this world and just because one might have had a few sips off the bottle before bearing witness to some of them, well that doesn't or shouldn't completely discount his story. I believe that science does know of the existence of the piggo and probably other "cryptids" as well but chooses to cover up their existence. It could be a pact that scientists have made with the aliens. "Keep it secret, keep it safe." The aliens tell them. If science were to admit to the existence of all of these animals, well, there's too much literature that would have to be re-written, isn't there? No one has time to go back and look at all the potentially mis-identified fossils and bones that have been sculpted into dinosaurs. It seems perfectly logical, after all, that a scientist finding a small fragment of fossilized bone can call it a hip bone and therefore sculpt an entire fictitious dino around that tiny fragment... that's all perfectly logical and sciencey... but to admit to the world that there are species in this great populated United States that haven't been properly discovered and studied... well that's just nonsense.

The Legend of the Suicide Queen

Not far outside a sleepy little village in Northeast Kansas there lies the remains of a small log cabin built on the side of the hill facing north. No one can report on the condition of the cabin as no one has seen it in a hundred and twenty years; at least no one that has lived to talk about it. Many people have gone to look for it, it's just barely off the road, through the dense woods and over a small rise, situated in a small valley, halfway up the hill, just below the cemetery. You can see the clearing on satellite images at latitude 39.5027 and longitude -95.8661 just south of 254 road half a mile west of Circleville and half a mile south on J Road. Just because it exists and can be seen from above does not mean that anyone should venture near it. Some things are best left alone. Many things are best forgotten.

When Ella Davenport was 15 in 1868, Kansas seemed like a foreign country. In fact, it almost was. Having only upgraded from a territory to a state 7 years before, it was a vast land of nothing to the west. Ella didn't go west, however, at least not far. She was newly married to Richard Davenport III and from St. Luis, they set out to claim some land in the newly formed state. She married young, but she married well. Richard and his two younger brothers set out on horseback with Ella in a wagon. Her parents had passed away just a few months prior and at her age, her choices were limited. She could marry Richard or head back east to live with her aunt in Philadelphia. Her parents had left her with a little money, not enough to live on her own by any means, but enough to get back East if she wanted. But Richard had asked for her hand and though she didn't intend to marry him until she was at least 17, circumstances being as they were shortened the courting period and they entered into an agreement. The original plan was for him to head west, build a house, start a small farm and then send for her when it was time. However, after the passing of her parents, it seemed only fitting that she pack her few things and use her little money to help finance the trek.

They traveled from St. Luis across Missouri and into Kansas, crossing the Missouri River five days before Ella's 16th birthday. They agreed that wherever they happened to be by noon on her birthday they would stop travelling and make their home, at least that's how the story goes. The plan was to build a small log cabin for Ella and Richard and another small cabin nearby for his two brothers. They also made plans for a stable, a barn, a corn crib and pasture for a few cows, maybe a chicken house, as well.

On September 2, Ella's birthday, they stopped just across the small river that runs on the west side of what is today Circleville, Kansas. There was fertile land near the creek and plenty of lumber for building. They set up a small camp and spent the next three days scouting the area for suitable location for a house. On the third day, they had decided to build close to the creek and started clearing timber. That night, however, a heavy rainstorm came through, the creek overflowed, and their camp was flooded. They spent the next day locating a spot a little further from the creek and a little further up the hill. It was Richard's brother David that found a clearing, halfway up the hill with a large level area. There would be no clearing of trees, there were plenty of rocky outcroppings nearby with chalky white Kansas limestone, perfect for building foundations. The clearing was surrounded by enormous white oak trees and Ella was in love with the spot from the first moment she saw it. It was the perfect size for a couple of small cabins and some outbuildings. It was close enough to the creek to walk but far enough up the hill to keep from being flooded. It was secluded in a large timber with mature trees. There was plenty of space for her to plant a kitchen garden in the spring. Not as though anything she planted there would have taken root; or if it did, it may have grown into something altogether evil. That place is a nexus, one of many that must spot the globe. It is a direct link to a dark and sinister power that men do not fully understand.

Winter came early that year and by late October, they had barely constructed the walls of the main cabin when the snow started to fall. They had few blankets or heavy clothes; little food and the nearest town was a two-day ride. One of their horses had eaten something poisonous and was near death. They had contemplated just killing it and eating it, but they didn't know if the meat would be poisoned or not. The rest of the horses refused to go anywhere near the clearing. They bucked, and Richard's brother Bucklin broke his right arm when he was thrown from his horse while trying to coax it into the area. In fact, they had never noticed, but there was never any wildlife in the clearing. There were no squirrels hiding nuts for the winter, there were no birds, no deer and no sign of any life at all. Had they arrived in spring, rather than in fall, they would have realized that not even vegetation grew in that clearing.

The Davenport boys were city folk, they didn't know how to build a cabin, let alone a house. They didn't know how to hunt or fish, and they didn't bring enough ammunition to get them through the winter. Ella was no better off. She caught pneumonia in November and Richard and David were forced to finish the cabin enough to get them through the winter.

That small clearing in the woods in the middle of nowhere was cursed. By Christmas Bucklin's arm was nearly healed and Ella was recovering, but David had fallen into a great depression. It was as if a darkness lived in that clearing where they were trying to build their futures. Before dawn on Christmas morning, David walked into the woods a small distance where the horses were tied up, he killed his horse and used the rope to hang himself from one of the huge oak trees at the edge of the clearing. When Richard got up and went outside to get wood for the fire, he saw the frozen body swinging in the winter wind. The ground was so frozen that they couldn't even bury him. They laid his body on the back side of the wood pile about 50 yards from the house to wait until the thaw, so they could bury him.

On New Year's morning Richard went outside to get wood for the fire only to find Bucklin's body swinging from the same branch of the same oak tree. His horse was also dead in the woods. Richard decided immediately that he and Ella would pack up that day and go to the nearest town to wait out the winter before they could head back to St. Luis. They were down to one horse and it was thin and weak. Things were looking grim. After Richard removed Bucklin's body from the tree and placed him neatly next to David behind the dwindling wood pile, he went inside to find his wife Ella nauseated and sweaty. She hadn't told him that she was pregnant. She wanted to, but the time hadn't been right, and this was too much stress to put on him now. In truth, she was six months along and even she didn't know for sure until the first of December. But something was wrong, and she was forced to tell him. He abandoned plans for leaving the cabin. They could eat the horses and they had enough wood to make it another month, they would pray for a miracle and as soon as the weather improved at all, they would make for town.

After two days of stomach cramps and nausea, it was clear to Ella that the baby was not ok. She begged Richard to ride to town and get help. The weather was frigid, but the wind had stopped and there was no threat of weather. Richard had buried plenty of horse meat in a snowbank just outside the door and he brought in enough wood to keep the fire going for a week. Ella would have to make due until he returned.

Richard never returned. His horse slipped on the ice while they were crossing the creek. The ice broke and the horse landed on top of him. He drowned in two feet of icy water just half a mile from the cabin.

Ella waited in vain, feeding the fire and eating as much as she could. She melted snow for water and the stomach pains worsened. After six days she knew something had happened and she also new that she was about to have the baby. She tried to do the math, she was just over six months along and there was almost no chance that her baby would survive. She would be forced to deliver her baby by herself.

The pressure was too much, and Ella decided that it would be best for both her and her child if she just took her life. She was too weak to hang herself from a tree. So, she took a knife, slit her wrists and sat down on the floor by the fireplace and waited for the darkness to take her. Just before she slipped into death, she felt a sudden urge to push.

The following March, a small group of hunters stumbled upon the cabin in the clearing. They were on horseback and when it became clear that the horses weren't going into the clearing, they left two men with the horses in the woods nearby and the other four went to the cabin. Before they even got to the cabin, they found Bucklin and David lying in the mud created by the freshly melted snow. The bodies were still mostly frozen. They approached the cabin only to find a large pile of still frozen meat just outside the door. Inside they found a dead woman by the fireplace, sitting in a pool of blood. There was a dead infant, tiny and frail about six feet away from her, still attached to its rotting cord. It was evident that the infant had been born as the woman died and it had crawled a few feet before perishing itself, its cord was wrapped around its neck. The blood was black and greasy.

A darkness crept into the men and a chill gripped them. One of them pulled his gun and put a bullet through his brain. He crumpled to the floor. Another ran for the door as two more gunshots sounded from inside the cabin. The last man was almost to the edge of the clearing, crawling on hands and knees, trying to escape the darkness that was pulling him to his death. The two men on the horses had heard the gunshots and were struggling to get the horses tied up so they could go investigate. They approached the clearing and saw their friend crawling towards them.

"Ride away!" he shouted at them. "Ride away and never come back!" And with those words, his hand pulled his revolver from its holster and he put a bullet through his own heart.

The two men mounted their horses, grabbed the ropes to the other four horses and rode away.

For a hundred years, no one disturbed that cabin. The bodies decomposed where they were, no animals, insects or worms dared to enter that clearing to feast on the flesh. The clothes rotted, and the bones froze each winter and thawed each spring. Snow, rain, ice, wind and gravity covered the cabin and pulled everything into the soft earth. The blazing summer sun burned the exposed bones and the fall leaves covered them in the stench of yearly decay. For a century, life went on outside of the clearing. Towns were built, farms were established. A cemetery was created nearby. The clearing lay undisturbed until three teens were cutting through the woods from Circleville to the cemetery and stumbled into the clearing.

It was the summer of 1969 and my mother was one of those teens. She tells the story even today as if it were yesterday. She was 16 and her friends Danny and Robert were taking her to the cemetery outside of town where they were meeting a couple other friends from the next town over. The cemetery was a popular meeting place for teens then, away from the prying eyes of the small-town neighbors. It was a mile walk on the road, but most of the time the kids cut through the woods. There was a trail that they usually followed, but this day was different. A storm had knocked down a huge tree blocking the trail and Danny had insisted that he knew another trail that would get them there.

When mom tells the story, she stops and fights back the tears. She stopped at the edge of the clearing when Danny and Robert walked into it. She felt something hold her back. They looked around and walked towards what was left of the old cabin, a pile of stones that had once been a fireplace, some foundation stones and a few remains of decaying logs. She remembers seeing skeletons nearby and she hid behind a tree. Something came over Danny and Robert. They stopped, turned and looked at her. Danny yelled for her to "Run" as he pulled out his switchblade and sliced Robert's throat before plunging it into his own heart. She screamed and ran back to town.

Four men from town followed the directions up to where my mother had told them to go. Only one came back, he never spoke another word in his life. After much discussion and deliberation, it was decided to build a fence around the clearing to keep people out. It may also have been intended to keep something fenced in.

A chain link fence went up and no trespassing signs were hung on it. No one bothered the clearing again for 20 years. After 20 years of frost heaves and fallen limbs, the fence was in a state of disrepair when another group of teens stumbled upon it. This time there were six boys, four brothers and their two cousins. They made it into the clearing and back home before succumbing to the darkness. The brothers told their parents at dinner that evening about the clearing and the skeletons and then all six boys went to the pool and drowned themselves. A few months after the funerals, the parents, being fairly new to the area inquired in town about the clearing. My mother who worked at the bank overheard their story and quickly the town elders had to decide what to do about the situation again.

A more permanent situation was called for this time and a local contractor was called in to build a concrete barrier, twenty feet high, in place of the old fence. A small road was cut into the woods and footings were dug for the wall. It cost the town an exorbitant amount of money, but it would be worth it if it spared the town more grief. The wall was never finished. The contractor quit half way through, having lost over half his crew to accidental deaths during a single incident one afternoon. The heavy equipment was removed during the night and the contractor was never seen again.

So, the town would rely on legend and myth to keep the curious away. A terrible name was given to the place. It was called "The Home of the Suicide Queen." Stories were told far and wide of a mysterious place in the woods outside of a quiet town that would swallow the souls of any that dared to enter. The locals preached the danger from the pulpits and from the school room podiums. Occasionally some out of towners would come by seeking the legend of the suicide queen and their cars would be found abandoned nearby. The locals would leave the cars for a few days and then have them towed away to the local impound yard. Missing persons reports were often traced back to the legend. There was even a television news crew that came out and interviewed some of us about it. We didn't dare tell them where it was for fear that they might try to investigate.

Eventually the story grew old, the small service road grew up to brush and each passing generation hears the legend with more deaf ears. But kids don't wander out into the woods these days, at least not like they used to. Country kids, even, don't go exploring like I did when I was a kid. The danger has diminished as kids become more attached to their gaming consoles and their phones and less attached to nature and her beauty and mystery.

Still, the story must be told. There is a danger in those woods and the one should never venture into that clearing, lest they suffer the fate of so many that have gone in before.

The Death of Mr. Simms
A Historical Drift

"Before I begin, I'd like to note that all of the official reports on this case have been deemed classified by some government office somewhere. Some office that I'm told doesn't exist. In preparation for today, I tried to track down all of the photographic evidence and official reports of my story, only to be told that none of it exists or ever happened. After all, officially, I'm dead. I died in a bus crash. But I can assure you that it all happened, and I can assure you that someone, somewhere is trying to keep me from telling this story which is why we're meeting under such unusual circumstances. I appreciate you taking the time to hear my case today, sir.

The first time I saw bigfoot, it was in my bedroom. In my bedroom, in my apartment in the middle of San Diego in a gated community. I was sleeping, and I became aware that someone was standing at the foot of the bed. Then I was aware that something was tugging on my foot. I thought it was my roommate, I thought he needed something. I switched on the lamp beside my bed and I screamed at the monster that filled the room. It was huge. The apartment had nine-foot ceilings and it had to stoop to fit in the room.

Its bulk was astounding, huge arms, huge barrel chest and thick black and brown fur everywhere. The light from the lamp startled it as well and it roared a deep guttural roar that shook the windows. For a moment, we were locked in a stare that made the world stand still. Time stopped as I saw its soul. That's when my roommate threw open the door to see what was going on. He screamed, and the monster broke the eye contact with me and slammed the door shut and grabbed me by the leg, throwing me against the wall. I crashed into the wall, breaking the sheetrock, breaking the studs in the wall and landing in the living room where my roommate was laying on the floor still, trying to get up. The monster tore through the wall and then vanished before our very eyes, its earth-shaking roar fading into nothingness.

I lay there trying to catch my breath, reeling in pain. My roommate moved to my side to see if I was ok. I had three broken ribs, a broken arm, dislocated shoulder, a concussion, a cracked hip and a perforated spleen. One of my ribs had punctured my lung. My face was a spider web of deep lacerations. There was blood everywhere. When the first responders arrived, they called the police saying it looked like a crime scene. The neighbors were questioned. The noise had woken up everyone in the building. The sound of the roar was deafening. The ease with which it threw me through a wall was unbelievable and had I not lived through it, I wouldn't have believed it.

When the police arrived, they found a pair of enormous muddy footprints in my bedroom, no sign of forced entry, and three hairs on the floor that they sent off to the lab. They had to cover their mouths because of the smell. I hadn't noticed the smell, but my roommate described it as pungent, skunk-like, and sort of like rotting flesh. No one could explain what had happened. My roommate had told the police everything he saw. I wasn't in any condition to give a statement, but I told them what I could remember a few days later when they came to the hospital.

It would be a month before we were allowed back into the apartment. I was three weeks in the hospital and a rehab center and my roommate was staying in a hotel. By the time we were allowed in, the maintenance crew had repaired the wall and cleaned the carpets, but the smell, though not as strong was still present. It was like a dozen wet, dirty dogs; musky and earthy. It was clear to everyone that we couldn't stay there.

We gathered what we could, and the leasing office was kind enough to help us find an apartment in a nearby apartment community run by the same company. We had just moved in and were getting settled when the police stopped by with three men in black suits. I was still using a cane to walk with at that time and my arm was still in a cast. My face was mired with a web of scars from where a splintered two by four had sliced it open. The hundreds of stitches had been removed a couple weeks prior, but I was still a mess.

The three men in black suits were introduced as FBI agents, though I don't recall seeing any badges. They wanted to hear the story for themselves. They listened intently, not interrupting. They looked at one of the officers with great disdain when he asked me a question halfway through the story. I had everyone's complete attention for the rest of the time. They didn't take notes, they didn't record anything, they didn't ask questions or offer any sort of explanation, they simply said 'thank you' when I was finished, and they got up and left with the officers.

I tried to get back to some normalcy of life, but it was hard. Something like that affects every aspect of your life. There were so many questions. I had night terrors, I couldn't go to work. My life took a downward spiral. Then things got really weird.

My roommate and I were coming home one evening after going to the movies. We both needed a distraction. I think he was as worked up about the entire situation as I was. As he pulled off the interstate and onto the street leading to our apartment, an enormous bulk of a monster stepped in front of the car. I recognized that guttural roar over the sound of screeching tires and crunching metal. That was the second time I saw bigfoot.

There were three witnesses that claimed our car collided with a 'monster' that disappeared from the street where it lay after our car struck it. It didn't get up and run away, it literally just vanished into thin air.

I was back in the hospital with another broken arm, sixty-five stitches in my head and a broken leg. My roommate wasn't as lucky, he was killed in the wreck. I didn't make it to his funeral, I was in surgery that day getting my leg screwed back together. The doctors say I'll never walk without at least a cane. Even today, the pain still keeps me awake at night. I go to rehab four times a week and I'm getting better, but still, I need the chair to get around mostly. I had to have my shoulder completely rebuilt too.

Do you mind if we take a break? I need a minute."

"We'll take a half hour recess, we will reconvene at 3:00."

… …

"If the court reporter is ready? Very well, we're back in session, please continue Mr. Simms, and I would remind you that while this may appear to be an informal hearing because we're in my chambers, you are still under oath. Your petition for support and to be placed under the protection of the federal government depends on your testimony today, please don't omit any details."

"It was when I was in the hospital that second time, after the wreck, when the three men in suits came to see me again. I remember more about this visit, there were no officers with them and when they came in, they pushed a chair against the door to prop it shut. They closed the blinds and turned off most of the lights in the room. I asked to see their badges this time, but they didn't respond. One stood by the door, another sat beside me on the bed and took my good hand in his. He didn't hold it like he was comforting me like my friends did. He held my wrist tightly as though he were checking my pulse. It was uncomfortable. The other one stood on the other side of the bed holding a black binder open. He flipped through pages and I could see that some of the pages were photos, but that's all I could see. Only one of them spoke, the one by the door. They were not as pleasant this time, they were abrupt, harsh and I felt threatened, even though they never issued any threats. I knew something was up though.

Anyway, they listened, and they looked at each other with concerned glances from time to time during my story.

I told them exactly what had happened. I didn't know then about the testimony of the witnesses. I'm sure they did, though. This time I could describe the smell; it was acrid, it burned my nostrils. It was overpowering and lingering. It was nauseating, as though a skunk had crawled into my nose. I could taste it.

After they left, I didn't get any more visitors. I got a few cards from friends, but no one stopped by my room. I spend weeks at the rehab hospital. My doctor recommended a therapist who came to visit three times a week. I was dealing with some serious guilt and confusion.

When I was released, I didn't have anywhere to go. My roommate's family came in and cleared out the apartment. They dropped off a couple suitcases of my clothes at the hospital and sold everything else to pay for the funeral and the bills at the apartment. So, I was free to go home, but I had no home, no money, nowhere to go and no way to get there. I sat in my wheelchair with my two suitcases of possessions outside the rehab hospital for a couple hours just trying to figure out what my options were. The social worker had suggested we contact my family, but they were a thousand miles away and we weren't on the best of terms, really. I assured her that I had a couple friends I could stay with, even though we both knew I was lying.

That couple of hours was the darkest time of my life thus far. I didn't know what was real, I had convinced myself that something else had happened and that the monster that attacked me in my room and then had stepped out in front of the car wasn't real. It was something that my mind had made up to fill in the gaps when I was blacked out. My therapist supported this. Still, in the bottom of my soul, I knew the truth. I couldn't explain it, but I knew exactly what had happened. My senses weren't dampened by the trauma, they were made more acute in the moment and time seemed to slow down. I could recount the sounds from the roar to the breaking of boards, the slicing of flesh, the screeching of tires, the sound of metal bending, the sound of breathing, the sound of my roommate drowning in his own blood, the sound of sirens. I could recall the sight of blood, mud, hair, the eyes of the monster, the lights flashing, the doctors assessing my condition, I could remember all of it. Most of all, I could remember that smell. It was like a skunk had been released in a room full of people smoking marijuana. That combination of cheap weed and rancid skunk was a memory I couldn't repress.

Eventually, I wheeled myself back inside the hospital to the pay phone in the lobby and I called my dad. I certainly didn't tell him what all had happened, just that I had been hurt and I needed to come home. He listened and then he told me to call him back in half an hour. I dialed again, and he told me to get to the bus station and my ticket would be there. Without money for a cab, I grabbed my suitcases as best I could, and I made my way the six blocks to the bus station. I'll be honest, with one arm in a cast, I didn't make it more than half a block on my own. A good Samaritan, a young business man in a suit pushed me the rest of the way telling me it was on his way anyway.

At this point there is a large blank space. With a little help, I managed to get on the bus, they left me in my wheelchair and put me in the very front where there was a place especially made for a handicapped person. I managed to wedge my suitcases between me and barricade that separated me from the front stairs and I fell asleep. It was supposed to be thirty-six hours on this bus, then I would transfer to another for the last twelve hours. Dad would then pick me up at the station.

I don't know how long I slept. I hadn't slept in weeks, I had napped. Between the pain and dreams, naps were as good as I could get. When I awoke, it was to the sound of screeching tires, shattering glass. I saw nothing. I had a feeling of being weightless as the bus careened out of control and rolled again and again into the ditch. I could hear tree trunks splintering as the bus slowly slid to a stop at the bottom of a deep forested ravine. All I saw was red when I opened my eyes. I knew immediately that while I wasn't seriously injured that I wasn't going to be walking away from this. I somehow managed to crawl away from the wreckage. It was night, it was cold, it was raining and still hurt from the last wreck, I couldn't manage to get far before I collapsed. As consciousness faded, I smelled burning rubber and that overpowering scent of skunk. I couldn't hear any screaming from any of the other passengers, I couldn't hear anything but the rain, the wind and then just as I passed out, that guttural roar. While I didn't see it this time, I know... I know it was there.

I didn't wake up for five days this time. I was strapped to a hospital bed. I could hear the now familiar sounds of the monitors and an IV pump. I struggled to see, I couldn't move my arms or legs and I remember wincing in pain when I tried to move my head. Everything was out of focus. That's when I realized I was blind in my left eye. My lips were cracked and dry. Breathing was excruciating, and I had a tube down my throat that was gagging me. I lay there for what seemed like hours just looking at a spot on the ceiling that followed my gaze no matter where I looked. I can still see that spot, I'm lucky I have any vision at all, I suppose. I should be thankful for eighty percent of my field of vision in one eye after everything that's happened. I should be thankful I only lost one finger and two toes. I should be thankful that my legs and arms are working again... sort of. There's feeling at least, that's progress.

After a long time, a young woman stood over me with a serious look on her face. She told me to blink once if I could hear her. I did, I think. She told me to blink twice if I knew where I was. I had no idea, but I think I must have blinked twice. She walked away, and I fell asleep. When I awoke next, the breathing tube was gone and there were three familiar faces in the room, dressed in familiar black suits. This time I could not tell them what happened. I could barely speak at all. One of them sat down on the bed and as both my arms were broken, he simply looked into my eyes. I could see him look past my eye, into my soul. It was very similar to that first night when I locked eyes with sasquatch in my bedroom. He held me with his gaze and told me only a very vague version of what had happened. The bus had crashed. I was the only survivor. For a long time, that's all I knew. I found out later that it was reported that there were no survivors. My family held a funeral for me without a body to bury.

I spent the next two months in the hospital, mending physically, mentally and emotionally. I was told at that time that my family had been notified but didn't seem care. I became aware that I wasn't in a regular hospital. At first there were small things that I noticed that were different, things that, had I not spent so much time in the hospital in the prior months, I probably wouldn't have noticed. My door didn't have a window. My room didn't have a window. My room was bigger than the usual hospital room and there was a door at the far end of the room past the restroom that led to a private rehab room. My bathroom didn't have the handicap bars in it either. I never heard any visitors or saw any other patients in the hallway. I was occasionally taken from my room down the main hallway and while there were other doors with numbers and files hanging on them, there was no nurses' station, no public restrooms, no water fountains, just white walls and brown doors.

In my condition, I couldn't really do much about it though. It wasn't until I escaped that I realized how strange the place really was."

"Mr. Simms, did you say you escaped?"

"If you can call it that, your honor. It wasn't much of an escape. I wasn't pursued. After a couple months of vigorous rehab and a daily schedule, there was a day when no one came to see me. I mean, no nurses or doctors came in. The red light on the security camera in my room was off and I went almost all day, sitting patently waiting for food or my therapist or something, but no one came."

"I'm going to interrupt you for a minute, Mr. Simms. To say you *escaped* implies you were being held against your will. Is that what you're saying? You were being held in this hospital? Against your will?"

"Looking back, knowing what I know now, yes, I'd say I escaped, but I see your point. Perhaps the word *left* would be more adequate. Towards late afternoon, I left. I got in my wheelchair and made my way out the door which was usually locked, and I wheeled down the hall looking for someone to tell me what was going on. There were no exit signs, so I didn't know which way I was going. I passed doors marked 'radiology,' 'cardiology,' 'biological studies,' 'specimen vault,' 'cryogenics,' 'eugenics,' and 'mythical research lab.' I really was curious about that last one, I remember, but I was hungry, and I moved on. Eventually I came to an elevator. I looked at the buttons inside. I was at floor 'negative three.' There was a button marked 'G' at the top of the list, so I pushed it and hoped for the best.

When the elevator opened, I was in a small lobby about ten-foot square with a single chair in it and a large metal door with an intercom system beside it. I wheeled toward the door and when it swung open the room was flooded with light. This was the first time I had seen the sun in two months. The outside air was fresh, and the light was blinding. There was a small pad of concrete just outside the door and a gravel driveway that led away from it. There was a tall chain link fence with a spiral barbed wire top on it, like you see around a prison compound. The only part of the building that was visible from the surface was the small building I had just come out of. It looked like a cheap metal clad building. Like the one my dad had put up in the back yard back home where he parked the van. The fenced in area was small and enclosed the small building and a short length of drive. There was a large gate that was open, and the gravel drive led into a forest. There were pine trees surrounding the entire place. I had no idea where I was. Not feeling confident about trying to maneuver my wheelchair down a gravel road, I turned to go back inside. The door had locked behind me, however and there was no response when I pressed the button next to the door.

With that, I resigned myself to the gravel. I hadn't gone more than 50 yards past the gate when I heard a vehicle approaching. The road stopped at the door I had just come out of, so there was no question as to where the vehicle was going. I tried to get off the road, thinking I might hide in the bushes, but my chair struck a rock and I tipped onto the gravel. The vehicle slowed, stopped and I heard a door open. I looked up to see three men in grey suits with sunglasses on. Even blinded in my one eye by the sun, I could still see that these were not my three friends in black suits. These were different men and I was quickly scooped up, blindfolded and locked into the back of a van that screeched around on the gravel road and barreled down the bumpy road.

For the next few hours I rode in complete silence. Finally, I felt a sharp prick in the back of my neck and fell into darkness.

When I woke up, I was in a room that smelled of dust, old leather and wood smoke. As I looked around, I saw an enormous library. There was a massive fireplace on one side and huge windows on the other with heavy dark drapes pulled to the sides. There was a large double door on one end of the room and the rest of the wall space was occupied by books, thousands of books. I was seated in a deep, dark brown leather chair beside a small table, facing a huge desk buried under stacks of books. That's where Dr. Paddin was sitting, reading. He looked up at me over thick glasses and smiled. He stood up and walked around towards me, sitting on the edge of the desk.

'You're lucky to be alive, I believe. Do you know what

a historical drift is?' Both the statement and the question rolled together into a single statement. I don't remember the exact conversations we had over the next few days, but I'll explain the events as best I can.

Basically, Dr. Paddin worked for a government agency that, of course, doesn't exist. He explained to me that it was his job to study mysterious happenings around the world, prehistoric creatures popping up mysteriously, alien and UFO sightings, religious artifacts and stuff like that. He showed me pictures of a pterodactyl shot down during the civil war, a brontosaurus extensively photographed by a drone in a swamp somewhere in a jungle in Africa, a picture of a prehistoric giant bird called an Argentavis shot down in Argentina in the 1930's and a plesiosaur caught off the coast of Japan. That's where I learned about historical drift. He told me of a Viking sword made with a technology that wouldn't be invented for 800 years after the sword was forged, stuff like that.

Basically, there are these like, wormholes that connect places or time periods, or both. Catastrophic events like meteor impacts, nuclear explosions or volcanic eruptions of great magnitude skewed the magnetic fields so much that they created these things called gravity quakes which are like ripples in time and space. So that bigfoot in my bedroom was a creature that was caught in some sort of temporal flux. Dr. Paddin explained that usually when these things occur, present day people may witness the historical drift, but interaction is rare because the drift existence is so fleeting. Sometimes the creatures are killed, sometimes encounters are extended, but usually they go mostly unnoticed by the world at large. However, since I had an interaction with the creature during that first encounter, I was, in essence pulled into a perpetual yo-yo effect and I now share a time – string with the creature which will continue to pull it to me from time to time. The men in black suits work for another agency and realized after our second encounter what was going on. They hoped to monitor me in hopes of another occurrence, so they could capture the creature. They were essentially holding me as bait in that facility in the woods, hoping to lure the monster. When Dr. Paddin's office caught wind that I was still alive, he sent a rescue team. When they found out that the rescue team was on the way, they abandoned the facility I was being held in.

I don't claim to understand this whole 'historical drift' crap, but at least it was some sort of explanation. I spent a few days explaining my experiences to Dr. Paddin who listened intently. That's when my fourth experience with bigfoot occurred.

We were in the library one afternoon, he was telling me about 'gigantopithecus' because he thought perhaps that's what this creature really was. I was pointing out the differences in the drawings in his book with details that I remembered when I smelled it. I stopped immediately and looked at him. He smelled it too. The color drained from my face and I slumped in my seat. I looked for my wheelchair, I wanted nothing more than to escape. He scurried to his desk and fumbled around in a drawer for a pistol. He was nervously trying to load the bullets into the gun when we heard the roar from the next room and then the double doors exploded into shards as the thing bounded into the library overturning tables and chairs. Books flew everywhere and the flame in the great fire place leapt up to greet several books that flew into the open flame. Sparks and burning pages flew into the room igniting the great rug that covered a good portion of the hardwood floor. Dr. Paddin dropped the gun as the great beast roared forward.

This was the first time I saw it in the day light. Even with one eye, I could see it clearly. Great dreadlocks of matted hair hung from its shoulders and all about its great body. The great mass was muscle, sinew and hair. Its great jaw opened, and its teeth bared as it roared with such force that I felt it in my feet. It saw the fire that was now spreading across the room and it threw a mighty arm in the direction of Dr. Paddin. The old man took the full force directly to the chest and I knew I heard his rib cage shatter inside his chest. His body sailed across the room, hit a bookshelf and crumpled to the floor under a barrage of falling books, knocked from their shelves by his impact. He lay, lifeless on the floor, his thick glasses in pieces beside him.

The great beast looked toward me and for a brief moment, we locked eyes and I saw his soul. I saw only fear and confusion. He had no idea what was happening to him. Locked in an eternal quantum leap, the only thing familiar to him now was me. He growled at me. He was so close I could smell its breath. The foul, rotting odor strewn forth from his gullet was nauseating. The fire behind me was growing exponentially and I could see the flames reflected in his eyes. I could smell the fear hanging on him like the moss growing in his fur. He turned for the windows as if to bolt from the room, but just like that, he was gone. He simply vanished before my eyes.

I, however, was three yards from my wheelchair in a burning room full of old books. I crawled and drug my body towards the windows. They were nearly floor to ceiling windows and the library was on the first floor of the building. I knew if I could break a window, I might survive this encounter. I didn't get the chance. Just as I managed to pick up a large paperweight off the floor that had previously been sitting on the desk under a pile of books and folders, the window opened and a man in a grey suit reached through the window from outside and pulled me to safety."

... ...

The court reporter had stopped thumping away at her machine some time ago. She stared at me with awe in her eyes. I realize that I'm not much to look at nowadays. I have scars across most of my face, including a great white line that sweeps across my left eye which is white and opaque with a singular red line across where the pupil should be a black dot. My hands are covered in scars from the burns. I do attract attention from most everyone. Most people are kind enough to smile and look the other way, saying a quick thanks to whatever god they believe in that they haven't been through whatever it is that I've been through.

The judge was looking at me intently, he hadn't noticed that the reporter had stopped typing. I stopped talking for a minute to reflect and try to collect my thoughts on how to explain how I had escaped certain death for a fourth time and made my way to where I was today, asking the government to recognize my existence and asking for support and protection.

"Mr. Simms, you bring death to everyone who tries to help you and to more who simply seem to be in the wrong time at the wrong time. That wrong place is anywhere you happen to be and that wrong time, well, I don't understand this historical drift concept that you're speaking of. Frankly, if you didn't have the scars to corroborate your story, I'd throw you in jail for wasting the time and resources of this court. I only half believe you anyway. I have no idea what to make of any of this."

"Your honor, I appreciate your position and if you let me finish, I think I can better explain my situation. I think you'll see that through the next two encounters with the beast I've begun to understand that the only way this ordeal truly ends is when the beast is dead, or when I am. The government has taken away my identity, I can't get a job, I can't get insurance, I can't get an apartment, I can't *live* without a judge signing an affidavit to recognize my existence."

"Did you say you've had two more encounters?"

"Yes sir."

"Judge?" The court reporter gasped putting her hand to her mouth. "Do you smell that? What is that? A skunk? I can taste it."

"Soon to be three more encounters, sir. Though I doubt any of us survive this one. My apologies." The roar in the next room was deafening. I closed my eye and waited for the end.

The Legend of Peg

I often think back on that night, the night I should have died. I still have the scar from where the knife pierced my right side, just under the ribs. It slid up into my lung, slicing my diaphragm muscle and causing my lungs to fill with blood. Had it not been for Peg, I would have been dead. I don't believe in God, but I do know that I witnessed a miracle. Some power that was not of this Earth was at play that night long ago. That night changed my life. It changed the lives of everyone in a small mid-western town where everybody knew everybody, except Peg. No one knew Peg.

I've worked many common place jobs, I sold cars, I watered plants at a nursery and I've worked at a gas station. Usually those were second jobs to supplement my income, so I could travel or do other stuff. I think everyone should work at a gas station job once and be exposed to all the crazy people that come through, all the stupid questions those crazy people ask and everyone, and I do mean everyone, should have to clean a public restroom once in their life.

My gas station job was part time. I was teaching during the day so I worked about 3 nights a week from 5 to 10 when the station closed. It was a small station, three aisles of groceries and candy, a long cooler on the back wall with beer, soda and microwave sandwiches. There were 4 pumps outside and I don't know how many times I had to run out and stop stupid people from pumping diesel fuel into their non-diesel cars.

In a small town, in a small store like ours, there was only one person working at a time, two during shift changes. I was janitor, cashier, fry cook, dishwasher, stockman, maintenance guy, window washer, floor scrubber, trash boy and accountant. I spent the bulk of the time just sitting on my ass at the small desk in the corner behind the counter reading or watching the cars drive by on the highway. Occasionally there were tumbleweeds that blew into town in front of a dust storm. We were right across the street from a hotel and right next to the emergency vehicle barn where the fire trucks and ambulances were kept. Once in a while there was some excitement.

There are always the travelers coming through town, stopping to pee and buy gas or ask stupid questions they already knew the answer to… "My GPS says 45 miles to the next big town, is that right?" "The sign says the men's room is outside and around the back of the building, you don't have one inside?" "The sign says this beef jerky is on sale for $5.99, does it ring up at that price?"

Then, there are the locals. You know them and their habits like you know the change to give back when someone gets a 32-ounce fountain refill and gives you a dollar… "49 cents is your change." The locals or townies come in all shapes, sizes and walks of life. You hear bare feet padding across the tiles (even though there's a sign that says no shirt, no shoes, no service) from the mom and her kids who spent the afternoon at the pool. She apologizes every time and says she will put on flip flops next time, though no one said anything to her about it and no one cares, and she never does. You hear the sloppy boots of the oil field workers tracking across my freshly mopped floor at 7:30 every night. They clomp in, grab some frozen foods, that super burrito bomb must be good, we sell out every day. Then they clomp out and cross the highway to the hotel. Cheryl comes in everyday at 5:45 to get a fountain drink. She cuts hair at the Hair Depot and she gets a new cup every time, but I always charge her for a refill. She pays with exact change and she flirts with me as she counts the change. I know she came in with that exact change in her hand already... no need to count it, it's there. The day the fountain refills went up in price drove Cheryl into a frenzy and I didn't see her for a week.

Clyde comes in every night at 9:00 for his six pack of Keystone beer. He's usually a quarter short on cash, but I'm almost always a dollar long on the till, so it's ok. He says he'll hit me back next time, but he never does and I don't care, I just work there. I was hourly, it's not worth it to stress over a quarter. There are 1,200 people in this town and I think I know most of them. I worked 5 hours, 3, maybe 4 days a week and I could tell you who was dating who and who was cheating on who and who had a fake ID so they could buy cigarettes and who wrecked their car last week and who stayed at whose house last night. That's the way small towns work. Everyone knows everything and everyone. Almost.

There's one local that you would only know if you worked the night shift at the Sinclair station. She came in at 2 minutes to closing every single night. She bought 3 packs of Camel Menthol lights 100's in the box, three small packages of powdered donuts, 2 chocolate bars (It seems to vary from night to night from the Dove bars to the Hershey's chocolate bar). She got a pint size carton of skim milk, and a bottle of water. She paid with 2 crisp 20 dollar bills and gets back one five dollar bill, three one dollar bills and 58 cents. I don't know what she did with the change, because she never used it to pay for anything, she always used two 20's. Everyone else that works nights always tried to close down before Peg came in. I understand why, she's not pleasant to talk to, or look at, or smell. No one knows where she came from, how long she has lived in town or how she lost her leg. Everyone knows she's homeless, sorta… she lives out of a storage unit just down the street from the gas station. The truths about her are few, the rumors about her, however, are without number.

No one knew how tall she was. There's a height chart on the inside of the front door so if we get robbed, we can see how tall the assailant is as he or she is fleeing the store. Peg hunches over most of the time though, so it's likely that she's taller than 4'7". She only has one leg and she doesn't wear a shoe. Her other leg is a wooden stump, like a pirate, I suppose. It looks like she cut it off a tree herself and carved it down into a club shape, I'm not even sure how high up it attaches to her leg, below the knee? At the hip? No clue. Rumor has it that she uses duct tape to attach it every morning. She walked with a cane, again, it looked like she ripped a limb off a tree and carved it with a butter knife into a splintery piece of firewood that she leaned heavily on. Peg has grey matted dreadlocks for hair. I've offered Cheryl a $20 bill if she will cut Peg's hair sometime, but Cheryl and Peg don't exist at the same time frame at the store. Cheryl is a 5:45 gal and Peg is a 9:58 type of person. Honestly, I don't even know if her name is Peg or if she got that name because of the peg leg. I've never seen her talk to anyone, she is always in the store all alone, no one has ever, ever come in while Peg is there.

Peg has a hole in her throat where she had a tracheotomy at one point in her life. She told me it was from when she died. What an odd thing to tell someone. It's an odd thing, she smokes through that hole and she keeps a small cork in it when she's not smoking. It's hard to see her eyes through the matted hair. She has the tiniest teeth I've ever seen in an elderly woman. The story is that she collects baby teeth from behind the dentist office and glues them into her gums, replacing them when they rot away. That's just hearsay... I don't know. Her toenails on her good foot are long like eagle's talons and tap on the floor when she walks. She uses the cane so there's a tap, tap of her cane and her peg leg then the tappity tap of her toe nails. I've never heard anything like it in my life. I watched her walk away some nights and I wondered what it sounds like on the asphalt of the highway she crosses to get back to her storage unit. I also wondered what sort of tracks she leaves in the gravel and sand that surrounds the storage facility.

I want to describe the laughter that I got from her when I joked with her. Everyone else seemed to be afraid of her, or annoyed by her, but I love Peg. I looked forward to seeing her and honestly, if it weren't for Peg, I probably would have quit that job after just a couple of weeks. But Peg... she's something to behold. I flirted with her just a little bit sometimes. I would call her "young lady" or "beautiful" and she laughed a little shy laugh that quickly turned into a cackle which then became an uncontrollable cough which usually ended up in a bloody ball of hair and snot splatting across the countertop. I would stand there as my stomach tried to empty it's contents all over the place, but she just reached over and used her coat sleeve to wipe it away. She reverted back to her shy laugh and grabbed her bag of goodies and her change and headed out the door. Tap, Tap, Tappity Tap.

I always walked Peg to the door. It would be closing time when she would leave, and I locked the doors behind her. Then I would go back inside and behind the counter. I turned off the open sign and turn off half the lights at the pump. I turned off all the inside lights, except the one directly above the small desk behind the counter. I typed in the series of key strokes on the register and the drawer comes flying out. I grabbed the till and the big bills and checks and cash bundles under it and closed the drawer. I rang out the register and closed it down, turned the pumps on "pay with card only" mode and I set the till and my paperwork on the desk to count down the deposit that would go into the bank in the morning. I sat in the office chair behind the desk that faces the plate glass windows. Peg would be leaning against the window smoking a cigarette, holding the small piece of cork in her other hand. She would stand there for quite some time, as if she were waiting for me to finish before she left. Sometimes I got the drawer counted down and the paperwork done and put in the drop safe before she would leave. Sometimes I looked up and she'd be gone, vanished into the darkness. Other times I heard a tap on the glass and she waved goodbye before hobbling into the night.

After the deposit is done, I still had to restock the cooler, clean the bathrooms and give the floors another wipe-down before I could leave. Often, it'd be midnight before I locked up the doors and headed for my car. The small town goes to bed at 9:00 with the exception of what I can only guess were call girls across the street at the motel, looking for temporary resident oil field workers to service. There's an occasional car or big rig that drives by, travelers who are trying to make it to the next big town 45 miles away before calling it a night. For the most part, the gas station was the last place open and we closed at 10:00. There's not much to do, so teenagers might go country cruising or drinking under the bridge just south of town.

For four years, I worked at that gas station. I got to know and was known by the locals. I did dishes, mopped floors, cleaned shit off the bathroom walls and listened to the town's gossip. Mostly, however, I waited each night for Peg to come in. I'll admit, I waited for all the wrong reasons. I wasn't anxious to see her, my heart didn't flutter, my knees didn't go weak. I didn't want to talk to her, or listen to her, I didn't want to watch the bugs crawling in and out of her filthy hair. I secretly just wanted to watch her. I was fascinated with her. How did someone like her really exist outside of movies or books? Sometimes I would ask one of the other employees or my boss about her, they would scoff and make comments: "wish she would get hit by a bus and put everyone out of their misery," "I keep a can of Lysol under the counter just for her," things like that. Nasty, hurtful things.

I should correct myself. At first, Peg was a novelty, a distraction, a fascination. Eventually, I started talking to Peg. She was married once, she had had a daughter. But as she put it, that was "in another lifetime." She used to clean houses for a living, in New York City, for the rich. She took a train out to the Midwest after her husband died. She hadn't heard from her daughter in decades, didn't even know if she was still alive. That was all before she "made a deal with the devil." So cryptic, I always just laughed and thought that was some sort of commentary on her lifestyle.

For four years, three or four nights a week, I saw Peg come into the store at 2 minutes to closing. And for four years, three or four nights a week, I handed her back the exact same change: one five dollar bill, three one dollar bills and 58 cents, and put those two crisp 20's in the till. During the summer, the heat and oppression of the day and her metal storage unit home made her stench unbearable. When it rained, she came in smelling of wet dog. In the winter, her bare foot was nearly blue. I offered to buy her some shoes, but she refused. I offered to take her home one particularly nasty night when the snow was blowing so hard you couldn't see the street lights just a few yards away. She refused and tap tap tappity, she hobbled out into the thick of it and disappeared into the blizzard.

She wasn't very talkative about herself. She would never tell me her real name. She never told me anything else about her daughter or her late husband. She told me that such things were "not permissible in conversation due to her current employment situation." I laughed at the thought of the idea. A job of some sort might explain the never-ending supply of super crisp twenty dollar bills, though.

One early spring night when she came in, she looked especially tired and worn down. I asked her if she was ok, but she didn't answer. She did her shopping and came to the counter with several items, but nothing that she normally got. A quart of 10w 20 motor oil, a frozen hamburger from the cooler, a diet grape soda and a package of wire ties lay before me on the counter. I couldn't even process what I was looking at. She stood there for a moment and I started to ring up her purchase.

"Wait, I forgot something." Tap, tap, tappity, she moved towards the back of the store near the beer section. For a few moments, I think she's pranking me. She stopped in front of the souvenir display and she grabs a t-shirt from the shelf. She calls from the back of the store in a scratchy, winy voice, "how much are these?"

"Eleven – twenty-five."

She hobbled back to the counter and I bagged up her items. I looked at the amount on the screen and almost faint. Without a word, she hands me two perfect 20's and I count back her change: one five-dollar bill, three one dollar bills and 58 cents.

"How did you…"

But she was already hobbling out the door. She moved faster than you might think.

As the time went on, I started to grow tired of working at the gas station. My personal life was in upheaval, I was just coming out of a 3-year relationship and I was looking at jobs in other, more exciting, if not more exotic places. I needed a fresh start. I hadn't really told anyone I was thinking about leaving town, I'd have to wait until the school year was over anyway, finish out this spring semester look for something else. Peg seemed to sense my life changes, however. She remarked, out of the blue, one night that my last night at the station would be a sad night for her.

"Did I tell you I was thinking about leaving?" I asked, thinking perhaps it had slipped out in conversation sometime.

"Sweetie," she said, "The end comes for all of us. But don't fret, you'll see me before you leave, and I'll make sure you make it out ok."

As the weeks wore on, I found a job out of town and I started making arrangements to move. I sold my house, I put in my notice and I started tying up loose ends. I almost dreaded telling Peg that I was leaving. I knew as well as she did that no one else in town or at the gas stationed liked her. I put it off as long as I could. On my last night at the store, 9:58 came and went without Peg. By the grace of God, I wouldn't have to tell her after all. Still, deep down, I wanted to say good bye. There was a longing in my heart to hear that throaty chuckle of hers one last time. That hideous cackle of a laugh that sounded like sand scraping her vocal cords was a sound that I had grown used to.

Perhaps she had heard I was leaving and was avoiding the good bye. Perhaps I was over thinking the entire situation. Anyway, I wasn't leaving town for another two weeks, I could swing by the station one evening around closing and say goodbye then. No big deal.

It was early May. The days were already hot, and the evenings brought a humidity that hung in the air like a dense fog. By 10:00, it was already dark and the stillness outside was eerie. I emptied the outside trash bins after closing and I went out and around the back of the store to clean the men's room. The heat and humidity were stifling. This was the Midwest, not some tropical hot spot... I swore under my breath about the stupid heat and I hurried about my chores outside. I unlocked the glass vestibule and hurried inside the store, locking the doors behind me. I retreated to the cooler where I refilled the shelves. Filling the cooler during the winter was a chore, no one wanted to spend much time in there, but tonight, it was a blessing.

Refreshed and ready to go home, I went back to the desk behind the counter. I closed out the register and started the bookwork before I went home. Tonight, was an unusual night, the usual opening shift girl was out of town and one of the new hires was opening the store the next morning. If you work at a gas station for any length of time, you realize quickly that employees come and go quickly. The pay is crap, the job is not exactly fun, and the average hire is looking to make a few bucks, then quit for whatever reason. There's never a shortage of applicants, however, who think they will stand behind the counter all day and count change. Once they learn about the joys of cleaning used condoms out of the plugged men's room toilets, they usually quit. Sometimes they don't make it that long. Often, they find themselves in a position where they can skim a few 20's out of the drop before it goes into the safe, or they forget there are video cameras and they get caught slipping a carton of cigs out of the store. For whatever reason (pick a reason, there are plenty) there is more turn-over at most gas stations than people realize. The fact that I had been there for four years made me a bit more trustworthy than the new girl was opening the next day for the first time. The difference tonight was that I was going to take the money bag to the bank with all the paperwork and drop it in the night deposit box. This wasn't the first time I had been asked to make the drop and it was on my way home. It took a couple extra minutes to put the overstuffed bank bag into the drop box at the bank. That saved the new hire from having to go in early and make the drop and it cleared my name in the event that she decided to skim out of my bag. This way my paperwork from my shift matched up with my deposit. In reality, I didn't know why the closing shift didn't always make the bank drop. It made more sense, but then again, I was hourly, I wasn't paid to make those decisions.

I took my time finishing my closing chores that night. It was my last night there and I guess I was feeling a little sentimental, or maybe I was thinking that a few more minutes on the clock meant a few more pennies on my check… It was just after midnight when I grabbed the money drop, turned out the remaining store lights and headed for the door.

I unlocked the glass door and stepped into the vestibule, I turned and locked the door behind me. It suddenly occurred to me that I would have to drop off my keys in the next couple days. I still had a pay check coming too, I could probably make it a one stop trip and take care of everything. I turned the key in the lock and pulled it out, then turned to the glass door of the vestibule. The vestibule though protected from the late afternoon sun was like a hot house. The heat was unbearable. I put my key in the slot and turned it. I pushed the money drop under my arm and stepped outside into the sweltering early summer heat. A bead of sweat trickled down my face immediately.

I closed the vestibule door and put my key in the lock. I turned the key and heard the familiar click of the mechanism inside. I turned around and faced the darkness. It was oppressive. The heat was like a dark blanket. My car would be a sweatbox. I suddenly wanted to be home in the air conditioning, standing in a cold shower. My mind drifted to the thought of Peg in a steel storage building with only a single door, no ventilation, no electricity, no air conditioning, no cold shower...

I knew the guy that owned the storage units. The bigger units had garage doors that opened up for easy access. The smaller ones, like the one that Peg lived in had only a small steel door. The man who owned the units told me once that it was illegal to rent the units to live in, but he felt bad for Peg. He also said she paid cash (all crisp 20's) for her rent and she had paid in advance for several years. That was a long time ago and I wondered if she looked like she did now back then, or if her present condition was the result of living in a storage unit.

I was about five yards from my car, the air was completely still. There wasn't a fly or a mosquito in the air. The bats that usually flew circles around the street lights and under the canopy of the station were nowhere to be seen. The moths and the cloud of small insects that they feasted on nightly were also in hiding. Nothing was moving tonight except me and I was dragging myself through the oppressive heat and darkness like a rowboat in a lake of molasses. The thick, hot air stifled the light from the street lamps and the canopy lights over the pumps as well. The shadows were thick like tar. The light did not penetrate the darkness. Normally, one could easily see my car parked behind the building, the outline would be visible in the shadows and the light would glint off of the windshield and the curves and angles of the vehicle. Tonight, however, it lay cloaked in complete and utter darkness. There was not room for parking behind the station, not pull in parking anyway. The alley was too close and too narrow for that. The employee of the station always just pulled up alongside the back of the store, their car facing down the alley. When I left, I always pulled around the store and exited onto the main street of town, it seemed easier than making my way down that creepy alley where the overhanging trees seemed to create a tunnel into complete horror.

I fumbled with my keys and found the key fob for the car. I pressed the button to unlock the doors and the lights automatically came on. I was still a couple yards away and facing the front of the car; I was blinded by the headlights and looked away towards the alley. It was at that moment that I felt a terrible pain in the back of my neck. Everything went dark and I fell to the ground, my keys falling into the gravel, my face hitting the mix of gravel and sand of the alley. The money bag that was in my arm fell beneath me. Barely conscious and not sure what happened, I felt a sharp pain in my right side and then I was kicked onto my back. Whoever had attacked me grabbed the money bag just as my car headlights shut off. I could see nothing. I lay there, trying to breathe, trying to regain my senses. My phone had hit the dirt with my keys, I couldn't find either. I tried to get up, but the horrific pain in my side told me that I wasn't going anywhere. I reached for my aching side, it was wet. I had been stabbed and kicked hard. I knew from my labored breathing that I probably had broken ribs, maybe a punctured lung. I knew I needed help. I tried to feel around for my phone and my keys, but I couldn't find either. I tried to see where the attacker was, but I could neither see nor hear them. I tried to call out for help, but the attacker, who was still very close kicked sand and dirt into my eyes, nose and mouth. I was choking and gasping in the darkness. I was bleeding badly, and it was hard to stay awake. I lay as still as I could and tried to listen. Hearing seemed to be the only sense I had available at the moment.

I could hear someone breathing. They were close, on my left. I felt like the car was on my right, probably only a few feet away. Useless without the keys, however. Maybe I could crawl to the car and if I could get in, I could blow the horn until someone came to see what the matter was, if I lived that long. I slowed my breathing, calmed my mind and listened again. I could hear the footsteps moving away on the left. I tried to open my eyes and through the dirt and the dust and the sand, I could make out a shadow nearing the gas pumps, walking away from me. I rubbed my eyes with dirty hands and the figure stopped. I could see them rummaging through the deposit bag. They just wanted the cash; the checks were useless to them and cash is untraceable. I knew there were just over $3,000 in bills in that bag, but I also knew that the money was not my priority right now. I heard a thump as he dropped the bag. Then the figure stood rigid and moved quickly into the deeper shadows by the building. Someone was coming.

I managed to turn myself onto my side, reaching across my chest with my left hand to apply pressure to the stab wound on my right side. Three black shadows ran across the parking lot toward the store. My attacker seeing that his friends had arrived stepped out and greeted them. They stood momentarily in the shadows and spoke silently, then they turned in my direction. At this point, I knew they were coming to make sure that I wasn't going to be around to identify them or tell anyone what happened. I was bleeding profusely, and I was coughing up a liquid I could only assume was blood. It was hard to keep my eyes open at this point.

The four dark masses stopped just a few feet away from me. Something behind them caught their attention. There was a faint noise in the darkness. One of them mumbled something inaudible, and they all stepped toward the deep shadow beside the building. The new arrival was past the canopy lights and into the shadow before I could make them out at all. They were moving slowly, there was a very distinct rhythm as they walked. Tap… Tap… tappity… tap… tap… tappity… Peg. I tried to call out to warn her, but I was choking, drowning in my own blood.

What happened next was a blur. When one nears death, the senses become very attuned. I could hear the wings of a mosquito buzzing nearby, attracted by the smell of blood. I could taste the sharpness of iron in my blood, I could see the glow of the end of Peg's cigarette as she inhaled through that hole in her throat. I could feel the hot earth beneath the side of my face, I could count the grains of sand that were plastered to my bloody face. I could see everything, the faces of the attackers, a singular bat whizzing around the canopy lights and I could see Peg. The four men pulled long knives out from their belts. They approached Peg slowly and silently. I could see them as clearly as if we were under the noon sun. I could see her face, she was looking at me, her tiny teeth forming a smile, her beady eyes reflecting the light from an unknown source. She was slowly walking toward me, seemingly unaware of the four men approaching her. Tap… tap… Tappity… Even when her foot hit the gravel and the sand off the pavement, that sound didn't change, nor did the rhythm. Tap... tap... tappity...

The first of the men reached Peg and I saw him raise his knife and make a stabbing motion. I expected to see her crumple to the ground, but she didn't. She spun on her wooden leg, her good leg swinging high in the air and her long talon like toe nails ripping the skin from the man's face. He screamed in agony, the knife flew into the air and he hit the ground. Without breaking her stride towards me, Peg caught the knife in complete darkness as it fell, and she plunged it into the heart of the second attacker. He dropped instantly, a cloud of thick dust filling the air. Tap... Tap... Tappity, she came closer to me as the third and fourth figures attacked in unison. Her cane moved with lightning speed, it's splintery length skewering the gut of the third man. She pulled it back, his entrails stringing out of his abdomen as his guts spilled into the sand. In the same movement, she flung herself into the air, her grey dreadlocks flailing in the barely visible light. She was well above the last man's head and she swung her wooden leg around striking him on the side of the neck, severing his spine. She landed with a light tap on the ground. Within mere seconds, she had killed three men and mortally wounded the fourth. Tap... Tap... tappity...

She slowly approached me and put her hand on the side of my face. I was very close to death and we both knew it. Her hand was very old, bony and rough. I had never come in contact with Peg before. Her touch was soothing, I could breathe again. The shallow bloody breaths grew deeper. The pain in my side lessoned. She smiled at me with her tiny little teeth, her hand still on my face, then she grimaced. I remember looking at her and realizing that she was taking my pain from me and claiming it as her own. I didn't recognize the miracle when it was happening, but I realize now, years later what happened. I think about it often.

"Help is on the way, sweetie." She cackled.

"You're an angel." I said weakly, looking into her back eyes.

"No, sweetie, I'm something else." She laughed, her voice was suddenly smooth as silk and her hand that was on my face seemed to grow youthful and soft.

I couldn't comprehend what had and was happening, I assumed that I was already dead, or that I was in some weird transitional state between life and death. Peg grasped her right side, her face grimaced in pain. Her breaths grew shallow and she coughed blood. Suddenly the parking lot was full of cars. First responders came from everywhere, the scene was suddenly flooded with light. My face was still covered in blood and caked with sand and dirt, my shirt was ripped from the stab wound and my blood was everywhere, but the wound was healed, a gnarly scar in its place.

X-Rays and CT scans would reveal the scarring from the stab wound, all the way to where the knife had scraped the membrane around my heart. There was never a medical explanation of how I survived, however.

The four attackers were dead. Peg lay in a growing pool of blood, her eyes dark and dull. My boss, the gas station owner and her husband pulled up and jumped out of the car in their pajamas. She ran to me before she even looked at the grisly scene that lay around me. Her husband, looking first at the carnage in the parking lot was spilling the contents of his stomach in the alley way.

In the aftermath of that evening, I was taken to the ER, weak and two units short of blood. Other than my new scar on my right side, there was no lasting physical damage. Peg was dead, a stab wound on her right side matching mine exactly in length. The four men were also dead. The police took down my statement, I told it to them just as I'm telling it now. No one called me a liar to my face, they wrote down everything that I said and they bagged the bodies. I got home around 6:00 the next morning and I promptly took a very long soak in the tub and then I slept for the better part of three days.

Never had such a small town seen so much commotion. I stayed in my house for a week, finishing my packing, more than ready for the movers to come and take my belongings to my new place two states away. My parents called, my ex called, the news people camped outside my house. My boss from the station finally stopped by to drop off my last paycheck. She was the first person I talked to since it happened. I brewed some tea and I told her the story again. As she was getting ready to leave, she hugged me and said she was thankful that I was alright. Business at the store had never been better, people were coming from hundreds of miles away to see the place. She was sure, however, that in a couple months things would calm down. We talked a little about where I was moving to and what I was going to be doing next and as she was just about out the door, I remembered that I still had keys to the gas station.

I reached for my key ring and slowly removed the ring that held the three keys to the business. As I separated them from the car and house keys, I saw a small shiny key on the ring that I didn't recognize. I handed her the three keys and I asked her if she had ever seen a key like this one, holding it out so she could see it.

She held the key in the light and squinted, "It says 'westside storage." She said. "It has a number on it." She looked at me and I looked at her. She was just past middle aged, maybe older, her oldest daughter was three years younger than me, but it was really hard to guess her age. She was tall, not thin, but not fat either. Sturdy is maybe the best word to describe her. She was kind to those she liked, but a royal bitch to those that crossed her. She was a perfect combination of business savvy and semi-compassionate, she was also my only friend in town right now.

An afternoon rainstorm was keeping the reporters camped in their news vehicles on the street, Linda and I formed a quick plan. She walked casually out the front door and hurried through the rain to her car. I snuck out the back door and into alley behind the house where she picked me up. She drove us to the storage units on the west side of town. I had been down the street adjacent to the units, but I had never driven through the gate into the maze of metal buildings. Each building had a large letter in the gable of each end and each door had a small number over top of it.

"Building B," I said, looking at the well-worn engraving on key.

The rain let up just as we pulled onto the concrete apron that ran the length of the building on either side. The rest of the lot was gravel and sand and right now, it was a muddy mess because of the rain.

"Clear to the end where the small doors are." I said pointing towards the far end. "Number 54."

She stopped the car and we both stared at the small door with the numbers 54 printed overtop. The door was non-descript, barren of any mark or decoration, just like all the rest of the doors. We sat there in silence for a long moment. I nervously turned the key over again and again in my fingers.

"How did this key get on my key ring?" I muttered, almost to myself.

"Whoever that old lady was... whatever she was, she was your friend and whatever she did for you, however she did it, she did this too. She wanted you to open that door."

"What do you suppose is in there?" I asked, hoping to prepare myself for whatever came next.

"Probably Narnia."

We both sat in silence and then we both broke into laughter knowing that in fact, it may be a real possibility and wouldn't shock either of us if Narnia truly was behind that door.

"You're coming with me." I said finally, and I opened the door.

Linda stepped out of the car and we both approached the door just as an old farm truck pulled up behind us. We turned to see Randy, the man that owned the storage unit complex. Before we could even say anything, he was out of the truck and walking briskly towards us, a folder of papers in his hand.

"If I weren't standing here watching it happen, I wouldn't believe it," he said, throwing a cigarette to the ground and mashing it with the toe of his boot. "Old Peg said you'd be the one to open er up, she left me a letter, mailed the day she died. Told me the day you'd be here and the time. Ten years ago, she paid her rent up to this very day. She give you the key?"

I held the key up in front of me. I looked at Linda and I looked at Randy.

"This here's as good as a will, she had the letter notarized and everything, I was headed to your house to give it to you, but I figured I'd stop by just on the chance that you'd actually be here. This whole damn thing is strange as hell, what they say she did and all…" he trailed off, realizing that the 'they' in his sentence was in fact 'me.' It's what 'I' said she did that had everyone talking. He bowed his head slightly, averting eye contact and he handed the letter to Linda.

"Everything inside belongs to you," Linda said scratching her head.

"Narnia is mine."

The key slid into the lock like it had been greased. The mechanism shifted as the key turned and knob turned freely. The door swung in and the darkness inside was bathed in light. Expecting the stench of human feces and rotting trash, I covered my mouth and nose. Instead, the faint acrid smell of dust greeted my nose. I peered into the darkness and then I stepped inside. Linda and Randy stepped inside but didn't go any further. On one side, stacked from floor to ceiling were bags and bags and bags of crisp, new twenty-dollar bills.

"You're rich," Linda said, inspecting a bag of cash. Randy just stood there, his attention didn't go to the hundreds of thousands of dollars. He noticed a small bag in the corner about the size of a bowling ball. He picked the old cloth bag a few inches off the ground, pulled out a small flashlight and looked inside. He immediately dropped the bag and ran outside. He hunched over and emptied his stomach in a mud puddle. Hundreds of tiny teeth scattered across the floor from the spilt bag.

No one ever saw Peg again. Not really anyway. There have been a few sightings now and again in cities across the country that sound similar, an old haggard of a woman who stopped a bank robbery in Texas by clawing the eyes out of the robbers, leaving them blind and bloody; another old beggar man in a wheelchair who managed to lift a city bus off of a pregnant woman. These stories make it to the news now and again, the media calls them Peg sightings, mysterious nobodies that appear out of nowhere to do miraculous things, they are always in the right place at the right time, etc. etc. Maybe it is Peg, coming and going in various forms. Maybe it's others who have struck bargains with dark powers for various reasons, coming forth to fulfil their part of a dark deal. There will never truly be another Peg. She was special. I kept the cash; the bank inspected every single crisp bill when I deposited them. Most of the money was invested, some donated to help the homeless, I could have retired and lived a happy life with all that cash, but I continued to work. I have lived a happy life. I've seen the world. I've supported hundreds of students as they furthered their education. I've lived my days to the fullest, knowing they should have been over long ago.

I think about Peg now and then, not the night she died, that's best forgotten, but I think about her and the warmth that she brought me. I only knew her for a short time, but she made an impact, the ugliest old thing I've ever seen, but the most beautiful soul I've ever met.

The stories about that night have never died. There's a sign as you drive into that small town now: "Peg crossing." A big garish sign with an old hunched lady with a cane crossing the street. It serves as a reminder to watch out for those who can't watch out for themselves. There's a small monument at the city park now, just a concrete pillar with a small plaque. There's a small urn on top that contains the ashes of Peg. I had the monument built, I paid for her cremation and when the monument was erected, I was the only one there aside from the three men that delivered and placed it on the concrete pad. The plaque says that Peg's leg is encased inside the pillar. I know that's not true. Just inside my front door is a tall cylindrical basket where I keep an umbrella, a walking stick and another oddly shaped stick that goes unnoticed most of the time. When I jab my umbrella down into the basket, it makes the sound that you might imagine it making if it were stuck into a small sack of pebbles. Those aren't pebbles.

Two Lost Boys
Finding Dad

The young kitten stalked its prey across the yard. Tall grass and unraked leaves made perfect places to crouch. Slowly, carefully, gracefully, Fluffy moved towards the grasshopper. The large hopper fat from a summer feasting in the garden. The small kitten crouched, and the wind blew a barrage of leaves from the tree to the yard where she lay in wait, flattened against the ground, tail out straight behind her, her long fur gently waving in the wind, her ears upright, alert, her calico spots breaking up the outline of her growing feline body. She sniffed the breeze, narrowed in on the hopper and took a couple short jumps forward avoiding the dry leaves that would give away her position. The fat hopper sat silently, poised on the concrete six or seven feet away, warming itself in the morning sun. A bit of dew clung to the grass and the fallen leaves; they made no noise as the kitten snuck through them. The newly fallen leaves would crack, and she knew the difference. She lay waiting, biding her time until she was sure the right time would come. Suddenly, from behind, her brother came bounding through the grass, crunching the dry leaves, taking huge leaps as he jumped over her hidden shape in the tall grass.

Butters bounded onto the concrete, tried to stop and turn around and rolled several times finally coming to rest where the grasshopper had been. Fluffy seized the opportunity not to pounce on the hopper which was now half way up the wall of the house, but to tackle her brother in retaliation of her lost prey. She bounded onto the concrete, a graceful, powerful frame of a half-grown cat, lean and strong, fast and silent, a stark contrast to her roly-poly brother. She jumped high in the air and Butters who had recovered watched her as she bounded towards him. He jumped as well but was caught by her presence mid-jump and landed on his side, his sister on top of him. He licked her fur, tasting the dew cold on his tongue. She went for a bite, not a real one, but a kitten nibble and they lay together in the sun on the warming concrete grooming each other, the prey forgotten, the morning before them.

I put out my cigarette, flicked the butt into the bushes by the porch, picked up my beer and went back in the house. Two more kittens were laying in the morning sun on the porch, dozing in a splayed pile. I smiled as I stepped over them. The momma cat was sitting by the door, waiting to get inside. She didn't enjoy the outdoors as much as her kittens. She wanted to curl up on the rug in the living room where the rays of sunshine would bathe her in radiance. When the kittens were inside, she would sleep on the top shelf of the bookcase in the bedroom where her babies couldn't quite get to yet. But now, the kittens were outside burning off energy and napping. She knew she could have a couple hours alone on the rug without the bother of the four fuzzy minions that she was raising.

I walked through the living room into the kitchen in

the back of the house. It was early on a Saturday, but the kids would be up soon, and they would expect breakfast before they went about their business chasing grasshoppers, cuddling kittens or playing in that huge cardboard box in the back yard.

I lit the stove and put a skillet on to heat up. I took another swig of beer and poured a little bit in the pan. I cracked a half dozen eggs into the skillet with the beer and with a fork, scrambled them. I grabbed the spatula out of the sink and started to move the eggs around the skillet, being careful not to let them stick to the bottom. The smell of eggs brought me back to my own childhood, to a time when my cares were focused on riding bikes down the dirt road or fishing in the pond at the bottom of the timber. The smell of burnt eggs brought me back to the here and now. I cussed and scraped the bottom of the skillet. I added some more beer and stirred it all together. I took the skillet off the stove and divided the eggs onto three plates, not evenly, leaving less on mine than for the boys.

The toast popped up and I scraped a bit of butter across the blackened surface. I wondered how one side always managed to get burned while the other barely browned at all. I buttered the burnt side to soften it and make it more edible. I set the three plates on the table and poured juice into two glassed and opened another beer. The grandfather clock in the living room made a great groaning sound and then started its 9:00 routine. Momma cat rolled over on the rug and stretched, her belly still fat from the milk that was still coming in. A month ago, she would have had five kittens contently purring and suckling from her, their paws massaging her belly, helping the milk flow. They still suckled every chance they got, but she was growing increasingly irritated with them and aside from the occasional mood of motherhood, she tended to stay away from them, distancing herself from their neediness. They were on dry food now and didn't need her milk.

There was no sound from the upstairs bedroom and the eggs were getting cold. I yelled up the stairs in an attempt to rouse the boys from their sleep, so they could eat and then my own parental duties would be done until they came in from play, dirty, sweaty and begging for lunch. Still nothing, not the sound of feet hitting the hardwood floors, not the sound of groaning about 5 more minutes, not anything. I decided five more minutes wouldn't hurt the eggs, I could always microwave them if they were too cold. The boys never complained about the food anyway, I knew they would sit, eat and be running out the door within minutes to enjoy their Saturday outside before the weather got too cold and they would be house bound for the weekends until spring.

After ten minutes, I yelled again. Again, nothing. The momma cat on the rug was irritated with my yelling. I had interrupted her sleep and she changed positions, curling into a ball, her fluffy tail flicked up over her ears. I started up the stairs to wake the boys. I skipped the third and seventh step by habit. They creaked severely and so often I was trying to ascend the stairs without waking everyone that I had formed the habit of skipping those two steps. I reached the hallway and my bare toes touched the rug. Even though there was plenty of light at this time of morning, I had grown accustomed to climbing the stairs in the dark and even in the daylight I sought out the sensory markers.

The rug, the newel post, the light switch on the wall where my right hand always lightly trailed. My hand reached the door frame to my bedroom and out of habit, I pushed the door halfway open and stepped inside. If the door opened any further, it squeaked, and I was always conscientious about making noises that might wake the boys.

I realized I wasn't headed to my bedroom and I paused for a moment thinking I could grab my slippers while I was in there. The nights were getting chilly, but the days were still warm enough that we didn't need to turn on the furnace yet. The old heater in the basement needed replaced, but that required more money than was available. Right now, priorities were feeding and keeping the boys in jeans without holes in the knees. The hardwood floors were cold to the touch, but slippers weren't needed yet. Besides, they made a swishing noise when I walked in them. No, I didn't need to be silent, I was after all going to wake the boys, but I still didn't see the need for the swishing sound just for the sake of comfort. The debate went on in my mind for longer than it needed to. I stood there half in the room, half in the hallway, one foot on the cold floor of my room, the other on the rug in the hall. The kittens could be heard down on the front porch, bounding and playing, hissing at each other in practice for meeting a foe. Fluffy and Butter and Kitty Poo and Tiger Pants were content to be let outside first thing in the morning to play. I always fed them now on the porch, not in the kitchen like I did when they were first starting on milk and soft food. There used to be Blacky as well, but she disappeared last week. She bounded out the door to the food dish and then to play. I watched her tumble off the porch steps as I smoked and drank my breakfast beer. When the rest of them came in to nap around noon, Blacky wasn't with them. I spent an hour looking for her, calling her and wondering, thinking she had fallen asleep somewhere and would reappear when she woke up, missing her siblings. But that was a week ago.

I backed into the hallway and trailed the wall with my hand down to Jacob's room. I closed my eyes and moved by feel, my fingers reaching the door frame. The old door didn't latch anymore since the house had shifted years ago. It was opened a crack and I could see the light from the nightlight glowing within. I pushed the door open and stepped inside. The small bed was empty. The light from the window shone brightly onto the pillow. The blankets looked as if some small child had just gotten out from under them and scurried away somewhere. Laundry littered the floor and chair in the corner, a glass that once held water sat on the nightstand, toys were everywhere, in the bed, on the floor, on the desk by the window. The room smelled old and dusty. I always loved old houses, the character, the history, the smells, the imperfections that you don't find in a new house. Old houses were homes. Thinking Jacob probably had gotten up in the night and went to sleep with his brother as he so often did, I quietly closed the door, leaving the same crack of an opening with the same glowing from the nightlight as it was when I first approached. I smiled knowing that in the next room both Jacob and Kev would be sound asleep in the bed. Kev kept an extra pillow on the bed for just this occasion. He was only two years older than Jacob, but he was the perfect gentleman of an older brother. I knew from experience that Jacob hogged blankets too, so I already knew that Kev would be curled up on the far side of the bed without a blanket, shivering in his sleep. His younger brother would be a tiny form under the huge comforter he had stolen from his brother. I stood in the hallway imagining the scene I would find. I would gently wake Kev first and send him down to his eggs before I dug the younger one out of the pile of blanket and pillow.

The door to Kev's room had a homemade sign on it. "No girls allowed." I looked at it for a minute and smiled. How long would it be before I opened this door one morning to find that he had snuck in a girlfriend? He wasn't even a teenager yet, but he was a cute kid and social and funny. I knew already he was going to be a lady's man. I knocked gently as if there was already an invasion of privacy by me just walking in. I pushed the door open and peered into the room. The bed was made, Kev was very particular about keeping a meticulous room. His clothes were put away and other than a dirty towel that didn't quite made it all the way into the hamper, his room was perfectly organized. His toys were arranged on the dresser in front of the mirror. His comb laid parallel to the front of the dresser, exactly two inches from the front edge. OCD wasn't something I was familiar with, but I had heard one of his teachers mention it once last year when he was in the fourth grade.

The boys weren't in the room. They had probably camped out in that box in the back yard. They did that sometimes, especially when they didn't have school the next day. It was clear they hadn't taken their blankets from their beds, or the pillows, I hoped for a moment they had taken the heavy quilt that was always folded and kept in the large chest in the living room at the end of the couch by the window. When their mother was alive, she collected quilts and while the valuable ones had been sold off to help pay the medical expenses, this old thick one seemed too tattered for sale. It was there for making blanket forts out of chairs and couch cushions. It also served for cuddling on the couch on chilly nights. More recently, it had been drug across the yard to the box where the quilt became all sorts of things. I walked back down the hallway to the stairs. I descended the stairs, skipping the squeaky two, I smiled as I wondered why I had skipped them this time. Clearly there was no one to awaken in the house other than Momma Cat who was no longer in a curled-up pile, but poised on her back, legs in the air, bent at the knees, tail reaching towards the window. Her soft underbelly inviting a scratch from me as I passed. I knew it was a false invitation though. I knew the danger of claws and teeth was real if I were to disturb her.

I didn't even look in the chest for the quilt, I didn't even put shoes on, I just pushed open the screen door and stepped into the cool morning air again. My track shorts clung to my legs and my thin t-shirt pressed against me from the breeze. Goose pimples appeared on my skin and I hoped the boys were warm and safe in the box. I imagined them curled up in that monster of a quilt, huddled together in the chilly air to keep warm. I imagined them safe and warm and I would take them both in my arms and be the father they had always wanted, strong, comforting, safe.

Three kittens scampered at my feet, hoping I was there to play with them. They seemed to have grown bored with one another. A fat grasshopper sat half way up the wall of the house, basking in the sun at a safe distance from the pouncing paws padding beneath him.

I walked across the concrete driveway and hit the wet

grass. It was cold to the touch and my feet instantly screamed with dissatisfaction. The kittens, now knowledgeable as to the discomfort of tall wet grass, stayed on the concrete and I made the trek to the box by myself.

This box, a gift from a neighbor weeks ago when their house had a power surge that burned out their old refrigerator, had captured the imagination of two young boys. They spent hours in that box, making it a house, a barn, a store, a school, a rocket ship, a pirate ship and who knows what else. It was a clever distraction from the recent death of their mother. Watching them play in the box was a distraction for me as well. I enjoyed the laughter and the singing, and I endured the occasional yelling and cussing at one another. We all grieved in our own way.

I stopped ten feet from the box and lit a cigarette. I coughed as the smoke mixed with the cold air in my lungs. I took a deep drag, letting the smoke fill my lungs completely and then blew it all out, straight up into the air. I watched it dissipate into the brisk breeze. I flicked the rest of the cigarette into the wet grass. There was no satisfaction in it and it occurred to me that it would be difficult to manage two boys, a heavy quilt and a cigarette on the way back to the house.

I stooped down, placing my bare knees in front of the box opening in the wet grass. I shivered briefly and lifted the flap of the box. The emptiness was complete. No crayons, no blanket, no toys, no quilt, no boys. They must be in the house after all, perhaps hiding from me, giggling in a closet huddled up telling each other to be quiet. Maybe they were under a bed, laughing because I hadn't thought to look there. They were great boys, but they could certainly be mischievous. I quickly made my way back towards the house. Two of the kittens were sitting on the driveway under the grasshopper, having spotted their prey, they were contemplating the logistics of now catching it. They left their quarry to chase my wet feet across the driveway. By the time I reached the porch, all four of them were on my heels, tumbling over each other in a fuzzy frenzy. I opened the screen door and they bounded into the living room, tackling Momma Cat. She meowed her disapproval at me but promptly went to bathing her brood as they tried to suckle from her drying teets. I could hear the purring from the kitchen where I went and sat down to finish my beer. I would wait the boys out. They would get hungry eventually and come clamoring to the table to eat. No doubt they had heard me yell at them twice already and were patiently waiting for me to come find them.

The eggs were getting colder, but the beer was getting warmer. I sipped, then gulped it, not wanting it to get ruined by getting too warm. I looked at the mess of eggs cooked in beer and served with burnt toast. Their mother would laugh at my attempt to make breakfast, scrape the plates into the trash and start over. She wasn't here though, and I suddenly missed her more than I realized. A tear trickled down my cheek, I wiped it away and put my face in my hands for a moment and gave into the emotion.

My eyes were red from tears when I looked up, suddenly aware that I wasn't alone in the kitchen. I felt them there before I really saw them. I strained through the tears to look at the boys. I wiped my eyes as I realized that it wasn't the boys standing by the doorway. My brother and his wife were there. Jack stood looking at me pitifully and Marci was holding Butter, the bubbly, yellow kitten. She was petting his belly, stroking his ears and he was purring loud enough for me to hear him across the room. Jack put his arm around her and I could see she was crying too. I realized something was wrong. I looked at their faces, fearing, feeling there was tragic news about to come to me. I started to get up and Marci quickly put down the kitten who wasn't ready to be down yet, and she bolted to me, encompassing me in a hug.

I looked at Jack for an explanation. His hands were in his pockets, his head down, but his eyes damp with tears looking at his wife holding me. Tears turned into sobs and I grew weak, I reached for the table to steady myself. I sat back down in the chair. A brief memory of loss shook me and I pushed it from my mind. I told myself that I was still mourning the loss of my wife. The couple months since her passing had been hard on all of us. I couldn't go back to work, there was no money coming in. The funeral was a blur and the boys, the boys wanted to know why God took mommy to heaven. I couldn't explain any of it to them. Where were my boys? I started to get up and I yelled for the boys to come down to breakfast. Jack came and sat down next me. It was then I realized he was wearing a suit and Marci was pulling the yellow cat hairs from her black dress. I didn't know what was going on, was I dreaming? I dreamed of Jan's funeral over and over again. It kept me up nights sometimes. I would stand in the doorways of the boys' rooms and watch them sleep, sometimes I would sit on the edge of their beds and listen to them breathe. Their breaths were youthful and free, not like the shallow dying breaths of their mother slowly suffocating as the cancer filled her lungs.

I yelled again for the boys. Where were they? Why weren't they coming for breakfast? Marci started picking up the plates and I snapped at her to leave them be. They boys would be hungry when they got up.

"They aren't getting up, Ben." Jack said in a soft voice through his own tears.

"Where are they?" I asked.

"We're here to take you to their funeral," Marci said, putting a hand on my shoulder.

"I need you to get dressed, man." Jack said. "Come on, lets go upstairs and get you ready."

I felt myself being led up the stairs. I didn't skip either of the squeaky steps and Momma cat meowed from beneath a pile of fuzzy kittens in the living room.

The next few hours felt like they were happening to someone else. Jack waited patiently as I showered and shaved. He helped me get dressed as Marci cleaned the kitchen downstairs. I heard her drop a glass on the floor and I could hear the shards and splinters scatter across the floorboards. I heard her cuss loudly and then rummage through the pantry to find the broom and dustpan. I looked at Jack, I didn't know what was going on. He worked with me softly, patiently, handing me first a shirt, then a tie, pants, a belt, socks, shoes, suit jacket, the whole time not making eye contact.

"Wake the boys," I said to him. "We can't be late to the service."

"They're already there, Ben." He said in a comforting voice.

"Oh yeah, thanks." I said, smiling.

I hurried down the stairs, skipping the two neglected

steps and stood in the living room. Marci came to the doorway from the kitchen and walked over, fixing my collar and straightening my tie. She did something to my hair and stepped back.

"I think that's as good as it's going to get." She said with faint approval of my outward appearance. She grimaced a little and said I smelled like a liquor cabinet.

I smiled my best Sunday smile and I looked at Jack who finally made it to the bottom of the stairs. He looked tired and old all of a sudden.

"What's wrong buddy?" I asked.

"Nothing. We ready?" He whispered.

The ride to the church was a blur of autumn colors in the window. I smiled at the kaleidoscope of colors in motion.

We arrived, and Marci opened my door. The pastor met us at the bottom of the steps and took my arm. I climbed the steps, skipping the third and seventh stairs. I didn't want to wake anyone in the church. It seemed like an occasion when silence should be observed. The front door opened with a loud squeal and I cringed at the sound. I peered inside, expecting to see church-goers looking at me with disdain over such a disruptive noise.

The pews were empty. I could hear Marci behind me telling her husband, my brother, he should walk down to the front with me. I hear him tell her to give me a few minutes by myself. I looked back at them, unsure of what I was supposed to do. Marci stepped forward, gave me a hug and whispered to me.

"Go on Ben, go on down there, your boys are waiting for you." Her voice was strong and sure but full of pain.

I smiled at her and turned around. I missed my boys

at breakfast and their game of hide and seek was about over. I felt her hand on my back and as if she pushed me gently, I started walking down the aisle. I stayed on the rug that ran the length of the aisle. I didn't want them to hear me coming. My right hand gently touched each pew as I walked by, I skipped the third and seventh ones, but I wasn't sure why.

At the end of the aisle, right in the middle were two large boxes. They weren't refrigerator boxes. They were clean, polished, beautiful boxes. I remembered seeing a similar box just weeks ago. These boxes were similar to the one that my wife was in. I looked at the boxes, smaller than my wife's, just big enough for the boys. I thought to myself that the boys would love to play in these boxes. I looked back down the aisle towards the door. Jack was standing there, Marci crying in his arms. The pastor was standing beside them looking in my direction.

I looked back to the boxes in front of me. A feeling started to well up inside me. It wasn't exactly anxiety, it wasn't pain, it was something else. There was some emotion creeping up from the depths of me and I was choking on it by the time I reached the first box. I reached out and touched it, it was smooth like glass. I could see my reflection in the polished surface. My face didn't even look like my own. I ran my right hand over the surface, I bent down and fogged it with my breath, then wiped the fog away with my jacket sleeve.

The door opened with that loud squeal and I looked back to see several people carrying arm loads of flowers entering the gallery. The pastor directed them up the sides of the church towards the front, giving them quieted directions about the placements for each bouquet.

I turned back to the boxes, conscious of the spectators. I knew that Jacob was in this first box, just waiting for me to open the lid so he could jump out at me. I imagined him leaping from the box and into my arms. He would throw his little arms around my neck and kiss me on the cheek and I would hug him and hold him and swing him around. Then I would open the other box and Kev would lay there, pretending to be asleep. I'd stand there looking at his boyish face, waiting for him to smile. He'd smile and then giggle with his eyes still closed and then I'd reach down and tickle him. I'd pick him up out of the box and with Jacob in one arm and Kev in the other, I'd walk out of this stuffy church with its silent pews and its overwhelming smell of lilies. This didn't even look like a church, it looked like a funeral.

At that point, I had a moment of clarity. My hand dropped from the casket of my son and I suddenly remembered everything that had happened. I dropped to my knees in front of the casket as the memories flooded my mind. It was just weeks after losing their mother, I had been sitting at home on the couch, a pile of overdue bills splayed on the coffee table in front of me, kittens sleeping in fuzzy piles in the chair nearby, their mother asleep upstairs on top of the bookcase. I had a beer in one hand and a cigarette in the other. I didn't normally smoke in the house, but the boys weren't home, and I didn't care. I heard the phone ring and I had assumed it would be another bill collector. Instead it was the hospital, asking me to come down to the emergency room immediately. I had looked at the clock, the boys should have been dropped off from school half an hour before.

At the hospital, they told me about the accident. The lady, her name was Rachel, who was kind enough to pick the boys up and drop them off each day had been hit from behind at a red light. Rachel's car had spun into the intersection only to be broadsided by a gravel truck. The driver of the car that hit her was a teenager on her way home from school, the police thought she was sending a text or taking a picture with her phone.

Rachel and Kev who was sitting right behind her in the back seat were likely killed instantly. Jacob died in my arms at the hospital. I was such a familiar feeling. My wife Jan had died in my arms just weeks before, in the same hospital, but in the cancer center, not the ER.

Here I was, kneeling in front of my sons' caskets. I had made them breakfast this morning. I had forgotten they had died four days ago. It was all coming to me now. The relatives, afraid to check in on me for fear of finding me dead with a suicide note nearby, the sympathy cards that I had stopped collecting from the mailbox, the casseroles, the cakes pouring in from neighbors and friends, the hugs and vacant words of sympathy.

That feeling welling up in me overwhelmed me now and I looked back towards the door. Marci saw the look of hurt on my face and she leapt from Jack's arms, rushing to comfort me. I was already on my knees, but I could feel my face hit the floor. The cold floorboards reminded me of the cold floor at home on my bare feet. A chilly autumn air filled my lungs and I couldn't breathe. The weight of the world had just fallen upon me and I couldn't move. I was crushed under the weight. One of the people arranging flowers dropped her plant and rushed to my side taking my hand. I remember seeing the concern in her eyes and I remember Marci calling my name. But after that, it was darkness.

When I opened my eyes again, my wife was sitting on the couch with the boys wrapped up in that huge tattered quilt. They were playing with the fluffy kittens, laughing and smiling. I got up from my chair and sat beside her, lifting a sleeping black kitten from its place beside its mother. The fur was soft and warm. The sound of a tiny purr permeated from deep down. My wife reached out and touched my face, her touch as real then as it ever was. My boys, hiding beneath the tattered quilt sprung out at me as if I hadn't seen them.

"Found you!"

A Really Safe Place

Gary awoke to the sound of his phone buzzing on the nightstand. He grabbed the phone and rolled over, almost pulling the charging cable out of the wall. He looked first at the time; 3:33 AM, then at the caller ID; Maggie. He slid his finger across the screen and put the phone to his ear.

"Hello," he said as he cleared his raspy throat.

"You have to run," she whispered into his ear.

Gary sat up straight in bed, fully awakened by the warning. He looked around the darkened hotel room, the neon "vacancy" light out by the office blinked steadily through the night and a shaft of alternating red and blue light from the sign peered through his window, between the curtains and provided the only light in the room.

"Where should I go?" He answered, his voice shaky.

"Come here, we'll go get the money and leave the country for a while." She responded, her voice sure and full of comfort.

He threw all his belongings into his bag, wiped his fingerprints off the door knobs and the tv remote and left the key on the table by the door. Maid service would clean the room again before the police ever showed up. It wasn't the police he was running from right now, though they would be on his trail within a few days. Right now, it was Rudy and his gang of thugs. Half of that money was supposed to go to them. They knew the heist went down without a hitch, that was all over the news. They also knew where Gary was supposed to leave their part of the money, but Maggie had talked him into keeping it all, stashing it and running. He wondered for a minute how they had tracked him down already, he had been careful the entire way. He avoided cameras, didn't use large bills or cards, rented the hotel room under an alias… he had done everything right.

He trusted Maggie, though. She was a sort of double agent in Rudy's gang. She should have been leading the gang, but Rudy was a bit of a brute when it came to leadership, so she used her finesse and her looks to run back hand schemes and steal from everyone. It was risky, but she was a smooth talker. She smooth talked Gary into helping her on this heist. She talked Rudy into letting Gary go it alone, if he had gotten caught on this huge take, there would be nothing to tie him back to Rudy. Bank robberies were a little bigger than what Rudy's gang usually went for, after all.

Gary, with his backpack tightly on his back, ran three blocks down to the train station. There he bought a ticket to Syracuse on the 4:45 commuter. He didn't wait around for the train though. He knew the cameras would see him buying a ticket and he purposely used his credit card. It was almost too sloppy, and he knew it, but he wanted to let everyone know that he was headed for Syracuse. Instead, he took a cab to the bus station and from there took the next bus to Atlantic City using another alias and paying with cash.

Gary had one of those 'everyman' faces. He was average

in almost every way- 5'9", 160 lbs, brown hair, brown eyes. He could grow a good beard if he wanted so he could pull off the Grizzly Adams, the millennial hipster, or he could go clean shaven and pull off the neo-Nazi skinhead. He blended into any crowd, always conscience to wear attire that didn't stand out in any way.

He hurried from the bus stop in Atlantic City and scuttled into an ally. He turned on his phone and called Maggie. He had turned off the location services for the phone before he left the hotel room. If it came down to it, the call records could be tracked down, but not the locations.

"Where are you now?" she asked with more anxiety in her voice than usual.

"I'm close." He replied. "I'll meet you at that pizza place near Atlantic Boulevard and North Indiana Avenue."

"On my way." She said, smiling to herself.

They met in front of the pizzeria and walked down the street to get breakfast.

"How did they find me?"

"I'm not sure," she responded. "One of Rudy's guys sent out a group message saying they knew you were in Philly and to start watching for you."

"So now what?" Gary asked, gulping down his pancakes.

"I say we pick up the cash and hit the border."

"It's too soon. That much money, you have to sit on it for a while, let the noise die down before picking it up," he said, downing his hot coffee so fast that it burned the back of his mouth.

"What do you suggest?" she asked.

Maggie was always the boss, for her to ask for suggestions was unheard of and it took Gary by surprise. It had been her idea to stash the cash somewhere mid-country on his drive back East. It had been her idea for Gary not to disclose, even to her, the location where he hid it; for his protection and for hers. For her to ask his opinion now threw Gary off guard.

"Let's leave it there and leave the country tonight. We can come back for it when it's safer," he said.

"Maybe we should check on it, move it if needed; before we leave," she suggested.

"No way! It's in a very safe place." He protested. "We shouldn't go near it for at least a year."

Maggie put both hands on the table, palms down. She looked at Gary square in the eyes. She pursed her lips and whispered. "We don't have the money to live off of for a year without it."

Gary, catching on that she meant to spend the money, not just check on it or move it, slowly reclined a bit in his seat, putting a much distance between her glare and himself as he could. They sat in silence for a long minute, a million scenarios playing out in each of their heads. Finally, she smiled and took a more relaxed pose. She avoided eye contact, stirred her coffee and stared at her half-eaten eggs.

"I just mean, we can't use anything that isn't cash right now," she said softly, control returning to her voice. "We can leave most of it there, take enough for a year on the road and come back later for the rest."

Gary nodded his head. He was beginning to run out of cash himself. He had a few hundred on his card, but that wouldn't do him any good, and that wouldn't last long on the run. It hadn't occurred to him that Maggie might be in the same situation.

"Alright," he said. "I'll take you to the place. We'll

get enough, and we'll grab one million and we'll skip the country."

They finished breakfast and walked out of the diner. Gary slung his backpack onto his back and Maggie reached over and grabbed his arm. She reached up a little and kissed him lightly on the cheek. "Where do you want to go?" She whispered.

"It's been my experience that money goes a lot further and it's easier to avoid the authorities in second or third world countries." He said very matter-of-factly.

"I've always wanted to see Mt. Kilimanjaro." She said.

"We have to make it to the money first," Gary said. "There's 1,300 miles to cover before we can even think about it."

"Thirteen hundred miles?" she gasped. "Where the devil did you leave it?"

"Its in a really safe place." He said. "After we get it, we can't just go buy a plane ticket, either. You can't stash a million stolen dollars in a checked back or a carry on and get on the plane, you know."

"We're not taking a plane." She whispered. "They watch planes and security is tight. We rent an RV with a fake ID, we drive to San Diego, we get on a cruise ship that goes through the Panama Canal and we get off in Fortaleza, Brazil. From there we take a boat across the Atlantic to Dakar, Senegal."

"You've suddenly really thought this through," he said trying to hide his amazement and his excitement.

"When you work in our line of work for as long as I have, you think about stuff like this," she responded.

"So where to then?" he said. "We have to get to Kansas, then to San Diego."

"I've already rented the RV, my bags are already in it."

"All I have is a change of clothes in my backpack," he said.

"We can buy you some more on the way, but for now, we need to get on the road."

They took a cab to a Walmart parking lot on the outskirts of town. Gary paid the cabbie and they grabbed his bag from the trunk. Maggie took out a set of keys from her pocket and walked toward the rented RV. It was a huge white monster of a vehicle with a picture of Yosemite National Park on it and with CRUISEAMERICA.COM written in huge letters across the bottom and again on the back.

Gary stood in shock, looking at the behemoth as she struggled to get the door unlocked.

"You can't be serious," he said shaking his head.

"It's perfect," she responded. "No one and I mean no one will suspect anything. Who in their right minds would drive across the country to retrieve stolen cash in something like this?"

Gary climbed inside and took a quick tour. Maggie's bag was laying on the bed as if thrown there quickly. He quickly threw his bag down beside it. She came up behind him and put her arms around his stomach, kissing him on the back of the neck.

"You ready for an adventure?" she asked.

He turned to her and smiled. He met her eyes and they kissed and embraced. She was older than him, he knew that. She could have been in her 50's, he didn't know. She had one of those faces that didn't age. You could tell him she was 25, and if it weren't for the fact that she had been doing this for over a decade, he would have believed you. She was seductive, beautiful and flirty. She was always in control, and she always got what she wanted, though sometimes she had to work a few people to get it. She was smart, cunning and had a way of getting other people to do her dirty work, keeping her hands clean. She talked Gary into making the biggest heist of his career fairly easily, but then he was young and eager. He was a smooth talker when he needed to be, but generally, he found he was most effective when he could remain silent. He didn't mind taking orders from her, she told him early on that she was going to take care of him, no matter what. He trusted her and that was saying a lot.

They ran into the Walmart store to grab a few groceries, some toiletry items and a change of clothes for Gary, then they were on the road. She drove first while Gary plotted out their route using the complementary atlas that came with the RV. He never told her a destination, he only told her to head for Topeka, Kansas. For three days they took turns driving. They parked at roadside parks or in parking lots at night. They laughed and talked about all the places in the world they wanted to see. At night they made love in the queen size bed in the back of the RV and then fell asleep in each other's arms.

As they pulled into Topeka, Maggie pulled off interstate 70 onto the Gage Boulevard exit. She drove a couple blocks and pulled the RV into Gage Park, coming to a stop in the parking lot of the zoo. It was early afternoon on a Tuesday, the park was almost empty. School was in session and people were at work. They got out of the RV and sat down at a nearby picnic table.

"How far from here?" she asked.

"Bout 45 minutes, maybe an hour," he said.

"Hard to imagine that within an hour we're going to be rich."

He smiled at her and grabbed her hand across the top of the table.

"Wanna grab some coffee first?" he asked.

At this, Maggie's eyes went big and round with surprise. "I thought you'd just want to get the money and get moving. You know, leave the scene of the crime behind and all. Where are we going, anyway?" she asked.

"It's a really safe place," Gary smiled. "Come on, then. I'll drive from here."

They drove north on highway 75 for 40 miles and then turned down a small highway labeled only and 'highway 9.' From there they drove a few miles west to a small town with no stop lights and a single little pay at the pump un-manned gas station. Gary turned the RV down a dusty gravel road at the gas station and followed it for several curvy, hilly miles until they came to a church sitting along the road all alone. The tiny clapboard structure was hardly used any more, it was still maintained, however by a few local ladies who met there for bible study once a month. The old sign out front with peeling paint stood between two mammoth cedar trees. It was barely legible now. 'Community Bible Church, the doors are always open, everyone is always welcomed.'

They sat in the RV for a moment, Gary smiling, Maggie staring at the small building.

"You hid the money in a church?" Maggie said finally.

"Not exactly. I hid the money under the church. It seemed like a really safe place," he said.

"What in the world possessed you to hide it here?" she asked.

"I went to church here for a couple years when I was placed with a foster family when I was 10."

"Are they still in the area?" Maggie asked, realizing she knew nothing of his past.

"Hell no, they died a long time ago when I burned down their house."

Saying nothing more, Gary got up and went back to get his bag from the back. He set it on the counter in the small kitchen area and took out a small flashlight. He opened the side door and motioned for Maggie to join him. She followed him through the freshly mowed grass to the back of the building. It was late afternoon now and it was hot and humid. A farm truck sped by on the road, they both looked back to see if it showed signs of slowing down, but the dust cloud that arose from the road didn't allow them to see anything. They could hear rocks hitting the side of the RV and they continued to the back of the building. There was a small hole in the old limestone foundation and Gary stuck his hand into the hole and pulled out a nail bar about a foot long. He then moved to the piece of plywood that was nailed into a wooden frame in the limestone foundation. This was the only entry under the building and Gary removed it quickly using the nail bar.

"It's under there," he smiled and shone his light under the building.

Maggie was on her knees, eyes wide with excitement.

She reached over and took his hand. Then she grabbed him by the back of the neck and passionately kissed him.

"I'll be right back," he said.

"That is a really safe place," she said as he crawled out of the hole with the huge duffle full of cash.

Two weeks later when Maggie didn't return the RV she had rented for 9 days, the company reported it missing. As soon as the police report was filed, it showed up in an impound yard in San Diego. It had been towed from a parking lot at 4th and Fir street across from the Quality Inn. It had been parked there, but no one had purchased a parking permit for it and after 3 days, the owner of the lot had it towed. The tow company had contacted the RV company and the RV company had attempted to contact Maggie, but since she had paid with a stolen card and used a fictitious name and phone number, they had not heard back from her. Eventually, the RV company and the police started to piece together that this was rented on a stolen card and a missing person report was filed for a Virginia L Elliott, Maggie's alias. Of course, this was part of Maggie's plan the entire time. The money was already in Brazil, being spent bill by bill on food, lodging, massages, and boat passage across the Atlantic. At the rate it was going, that money would last a lifetime.

Back in Kansas, a local teenager was mowing the yard of the old clapboard church and the smell of something dead followed him as he moved around the building. Thinking a raccoon or feral cat had crawled under the building and died, he removed the small plywood panel on the back of the building. He peered into the darkness. It looked as though something had recently disturbed the dirt near the panel, so he went to his truck to get a flashlight. As he looked underneath, he could see that something large had been under there recently, but he couldn't see anything else.

Two days later, four older ladies walked into the building for their bible study. They opened the windows to let in the morning breeze but the smell of death was so strong on the air that they closed the windows and moved to Margaret's parlor for their meeting since she lived just down the road. Margaret's husband, a local farmer, came home for lunch to find the old ladies gossiping in the front room of the house, drinking coffee and eating freshly made cakes. Margaret explained to him about the smell at the church and since Ralph owned the land surrounding the old church, he wondered if perhaps one of his cows in that pasture had died and he went to investigate.

As Ralph got out of his dusty old Dodge pickup in front of the church and slammed the door, he was met with that pungent smell of decay. He crossed the fence into the pasture trying to locate the odor, but finally determined the smell was coming from the church itself. He walked into the building and the odor was like a brick wall. He covered his mouth and nose and looked around. He finally decided a wild animal had gotten into the attic of the building and died. Left alone with a window open, the smell would go away in a couple weeks. He cracked two windows, one on either side of the building and walked away.

Many years ago, the bell had been taken out of the church and put on display in the front yard. The old ropes from the tower lay unused, coiled in a small room above the foyer of the church. Just a year before the church stopped having regular weekly meetings due to a decline in the congregation, a drop ceiling had been installed throughout the entire building. In the foyer, this drop ceiling covered the trapdoor that led up to the old bell tower. Had anyone really looked, they would have noticed a scratch on the floor beneath where that trap door was. A chair had been placed there, the ceiling tile had been removed, the trap door opened, and a body hoisted into the small room that used to house the bell.

It was years later when the church was being moved into a small town nearby to serve as a museum for the county historical society that someone opened that trapdoor. The smell had long since gone away, the meat and flesh had rotted away, and the skeleton had at some point, after the tendons, muscles and sinew could no longer hold it together, fallen. When the trapdoor was moved, a couple bones fell to the foyer floor. The police were called in to investigate, but they were as stumped as the locals. They called the body Jane Doe and decided she died from being beaten on the back of the head by something like a nail bar.

The sheriff, looking over the situation and scratching his head muttered to his deputy, "Man, what a place to hide a body. That's a really safe place."

Printed in the United States
By Bookmasters